Sensible RETRIBUTION

JENNY TAYLOR

ISBN 979-8-88540-500-3 (paperback)
ISBN 979-8-88540-502-7 (hardcover)
ISBN 979-8-88540-501-0 (digital)

Christian Faith Publishing
832 Park Avenue
Meadville, PA 16335
www.christianfaithpublishing.com

Printed in the United States of America

Contents

1

The Funeral

It is the year of our Lord 1794.

"Sir Linton, Miss Isabella, good morning. Please follow me."

"Thank you, Mr. Acton," said Sir Linton.

"Papa, you know I did not want to attend. I have not been to any funeral since Mum died," said Isabella.

"I understand, dearest, but it is to our advantage and my responsibility to attend Mrs. Ferrars's funeral. Isabella, look around, my dear. Do you not feel the thickness in the air? Such polite disregard among this tribe."

"Yes, Papa. It is as cold and gloomy in here as it is outdoors."

"Dearest, I want you to observe and learn more about this family. Some are the epitome of greed, snobbery, manipulation, and deceit while the rest have their peace and reclamation or soon will. Look at the first row, Isabella. What do you see?"

"I see Edward, Elinor, Kennedi, and Brody. In the row behind, I see Robert, Lucy, John, and Fanny. Has rank been disregarded, Papa?"

"No, dearest, it has been restored. Mrs. Ferrars was completely aware that her family's situations were planted and tended to by her alone years ago."

"Isabella, if you are going to follow in my footsteps, then you must completely understand all the players involved and their evolutionary process."

1

"You must know a great deal about this family and their secrets, Papa."

"Yes, dearest, I do. My knowledge affords me the opportunity to give guidance through legal and monetary distributions. I apply myself with every client I have. The fact that I'm called the 'gate-keeper' proves my standing and great success in the legal and financial occupation. Years of hard work and dedication have afforded us great luxuries for which humility must be maintained. Isabella, you have slowly become part of this family's legacy due to your friendships."

"Me, part of the Ferrars's legacy? How interesting. I too shall immerse myself in your work. What else need I understand about Mrs. Ferrars, Papa?"

"We will discuss this further after we get home from her funeral. I have an interview at two o'clock with Mrs. Ferrars's children for the reading of her will. It should make for an interesting afternoon. Looks like Father Williams has concluded the service. Let's give our condolences and then go home."

"Papa, now that we have concluded our dinner, may we have our discussion?"

"Certainly, my dear. In order to understand Mrs. Ferrars's children, you must understand Mrs. Ferrars. In keeping with this discussion, I must have your confidence that this information remains between us."

"Of course, Papa. I am fully aware of the importance of your occupation."

"Excellent. Let's begin then. Evelynn Ferrars grew up in wealth and status through her father. Edward Sommers was very fond of Evelynn and showered her with gifts rather than of himself. Evelynn mistakenly thought the gifts were given in love. Her mother was of peculiar persuasions. Not much affection, if any, was given to Evelynn by her mother. Instead, her mother relied heavily on their governess and her husband to raise Evelynn. The mother was much involved in her own status and parties with good society.

"As Evelynn grew up, her mother began to show her attention—the attention not for sake of love but of grooming into attaining and conducting oneself into elite society. Evelynn had an idea of what love is because of her friend's parents next door. They lacked nothing and still had the attachment of their parents. Evelynn had done everything right according to polite society. At the age of eighteen, Evelynn met a man ten years her senior.

"Jackson Edward Ferrars was a man of status and wealth. He was a fine doctor who was given the nickname "the gentle giant." He came to know Evelynn at one of her mother's elite parties. An attachment had formed between Jackson Edward Ferrars and Evelynn."

"Did she finally find love, Papa?"

"Well, my dear, it was her version of love. It is all she knew and lived by. Evelynn married Jackson Ferrars. They remained married despite the lack of true love from Evelynn. Mrs. Ferrars endeavored to maintain her status in her current situation. She made sure their house was large, staff was many, and social standing complete—all apart from the notion of love.

"One fine day, Mr. Ferrars desired a discussion with Evelynn over family matters. As Evelynn sat on the new davenport, her mind wondered to a social gathering on Saturday next.

'My dear Evelynn, are you with me?'

'Yes, Mr. Ferrars, forgive me.'

'Mrs. Ferrars, we have been married for a year, and we still have no children. My profession affords me the ability to bring many children into our society, and yet I am wanting children of my own. Do you not have the desire to have children with me?'

'Forgive me Mr. Ferrars, I have been much engaged in settling our home this year. I reproach myself in not fulfilling our understanding and will conduct myself to extending our lineage.'

'Thank you, my dear. I am delighted in the notion of filling our home with love and children.'

"Within the year, Evelynn had finally given her husband a baby boy.

'Mr. Ferrars, we have a son. What shall we call him?'

'Thank you, my dear, for this blessing. I have always been agreeable to the name *Edward*. I believe it suits him perfectly.'

"Within the next four years, Evelynn had given her husband a daughter, whom they named Fanny, and another son, who was

3

called Robert. Raising three children would prove to be difficult, so of course, three separate governesses were to be employed.

"Evelynn couldn't—or I should say wouldn't—find the time to interact that much with her children during their infancy stage. She stayed very active with her social obligations. Mr. Ferrars did spend what little time he had with his children, especially Edward, his namesake and firstborn.

"As time carried on, the differences between Edward and his siblings became very apparent. Edward took on a caring, giving, and shy personality, much like his father, making him a better person apart from his siblings.

"Fanny and Robert were conducted on a different path. Evelynn thought it necessary to educate them about the life elite. Love didn't seep into Fanny or Robert through their mother, instead mirroring Evelynn's life with her mother. Each child carried their learned personality into adulthood, thanks to their parents, be it good or bad.

"While the children were in their teen years, tragedy struck. Mr. Ferrars died from an apparent heart attack. This tragedy might have given rise to a solemn climate within the Ferrars's home if it wasn't for Evelynn. She stood strong because perception was everything to her. Evelynn showed no weakness—not even to her own children. Her main concern now was to ensure that the funds would continue after Mr. Ferrars's death.

"Edward had a different situation. His loving and caring nature was passed onto him by his dear father. He desperately clung to the memory of his father. Who would he turn to now for love? He was certain that his mother, sister, or brother would not be there for him in support of him mourning their father."

"Papa, I now understand why the Ferrars children are a mirror image of their respective parents," remarked Isabella.

"Yes, dearest, their situation is both happy and sorrowful. Did you notice out of the three who has children?" asked Sir Linton.

"Edward is the only one, Papa. He and Elinor have two children, Kennedi and Brody."

"I have been to their home many times and have seen and felt the love among them."

"As have I, Isabella. I desire that you only surround yourself with affectionate people but realize that it is not always possible. We must conclude our discussion for now because the Ferrars and Dashwood families will be descending upon us soon."

"Papa, do you want me to stay here with you while you read the will?"

"Yes, Isabella. You are not only my daughter but my apprentice."

"What if the family have an objection to my presence?"

"There is no recourse against me for you being present. I have already had this same discussion with Mrs. Ferrars while drafting her will. She has given me her permission for you, Isabella Linton, to be present at the reading. I explained to Mrs. Ferrars that you are my apprentice as well as my daughter."

"What did she say about that, Papa?"

"She was humorous for a moment. I thought her eyes were going to leap out from their sockets and roll into the great hall. She finally sat back into the chair and gave me a strange smile of acceptance and satisfaction. I believe she felt as if she was contributing to your future in some small way. Isabella, we do need to establish some procedure for all reading of wills."

"Like what, Papa?"

"First, when we are occupied in my office, you must address me as Sir Linton, and I shall address you as Miss Linton. Next, you shall stand beside me on my right side and hand me any manner of documents needed."

"Thank you for guiding me, Papa—I mean Sir Linton. I hear the bell, Papa."

"Yes, dearest, the tribe has arrived. I want you to meet them in the great hall and bring them to my office. As you show them in, allow them to sit where they desire."

"Why, Papa—I mean Sir Linton?"

"I am curious as to where they will place themselves, Miss Linton."

"Ahh, more study of this family, Sir Linton?"

"Indeed, Miss Linton, indeed."

2

The Will

Arrival of family for will

"Good afternoon, Mr. and Mrs. Dashwood, Robert, Lucy, Edward, and Elinor. Please be seated," said Sir Linton. "Miss Linton, please bring me the documents necessary for our discussion."

"Here it is, Sir Linton."

"Thank you, Miss Linton."

"I shall call Miss Wall to get us some tea for refreshment," said Isabella.

"Thank you, Miss Linton," said Sir Linton.

At that moment, Fanny Dashwood, making herself matriarch of the family, spoke up with no reservation. "Sir Linton, may I inquire as to the presence of Miss Linton?"

"Why, of course, you may, Mrs. Dashwood. Miss Linton is my apprentice and is present to assist me to carry out the reading of your mother's will."

"Your apprentice! Is she not your daughter?" asked Mrs. Dashwood.

"Yes, on both counts, Mrs. Dashwood. Is there an objection?"

Fanny, perched on the edge of her seat, responds, "I think it inappropriate for any young lady to be involved in such affairs."

At that moment, Miss Linton showed Miss Wall, Isabella's governess, in with the tea.

6

"Set the tea here, Miss Wall, and thank you." Isabella proceeded to distribute the tea to the family.

"Your mother was fully aware of Miss Linton's involvement in this matter and gave her consent for her to be involved. I have it documented on an agreement—if you desire to see it?"

"No, Sir Linton, I shall be in agreement…for now," said Fanny.

Isabella returned to her papa's right side, beaming with pride.

"Excellent, we shall begin. We want to offer our condolences to your family for the loss of your mother. Evelynn Ferrars came to me six months ago with a clear understanding of how she wanted her will to be stated.

"I have represented your family in all matters for many years as my father before me. I ask that you all sit in repose as I read aloud her will with no interruptions. I have made validated copies of your mother's will for each of your respective families. Miss Linton will distribute them accordingly when our time has ended. I will expect you to make an interview with me at a later time should you have any further inquiry about her will."

Isabella stood still in anticipation of any grumbling or issues associated with the reading of this will.

"Let us continue to the will then," said Sir Linton.

Will and Testament for Mrs. Evelynn Ferrars
15, October 1794

I Evelynn Ferrars, presently of 1400 Westbury street, London, England, hereby revoke all former testamentary dispositions made by me and declare this document to be my last will and testament. I revoke all prior wills and codicils. I am not married, but a widow.

I should desire to leave all of my jewellery to my granddaughter, Kennedi Ferrars.

I should desire to leave all of my equestrian articles as well as my horse Max, to my grandson Brody Ferrars.

I should desire to leave all of my linens, books, china, and silver to my daughter-in-law Elinor Ferrars.

I should desire to leave fifty thousand pounds, along with my two prized remaining horses, Silver, and Gold, to my son Edward C. Ferrars.

I should desire to leave my son, Robert Ferrars and daughter-in-law Lucy Ferrars my barouche.

I should desire to leave my daughter, Fanny F. Dashwood and son-in-law, John Dashwood my imperial davenport.

I should desire what is left of my estate to be sold. The monies there from to be given to my debtors and remaining monies to my church, Saint Mark church in Chelsea, England.

Debtors are to be paid 19,124 pounds as declared.

Remaining monies in the amount of twenty thousand pounds as declared, awarded to Saint Mark's Church in Chelsea, England.

I should desire that my home at 1400 Westburry Street in London, England be used as an institution for the learning of underprivileged young ladies. Along with a stipend of twenty-five thousand pounds. The afore mentioned home is clear of debt. It will be managed by Sir Philip Linton.

In conclusion, I, Evelynn Ferrars, being of sound mind acknowledge the fullness of my will. My Executor Sir Philip Linton, shall carry out my desires to the letter, as he has been my barrister for many years and I give him my full authority and confidence.

I desire no oppositional discussions as to the final and complete information in this, my will.

I desire that each one of you mentioned in this, my will, reflect and understand, in your minds, the reasons for your gifts.

May you all be content and filled with affection for all time. My life was mainly content, but also filled with much regret.

"This will was witnessed by Sir Maxwell Baker, Sir Alton Morow and myself along with your mothers signing on 15, October, 1794.

As Isabella stood quietly on her papa's right side during the reading of the will, she was astonished. She observed Fanny and Robert especially. She thought they would leap from their chairs. Their faces seemed to contort with each sentence read. It was shameful the way they were presenting themselves. Isabella now truly understood that their conduct was generational and sorrowful. She was glad to see that Edward's and Elinor's quiet reactions were heartfelt. Their reaction proved that love and caring can exist as long as they had someone to show them the path.

Lucy was a bit perplexing, for she was sitting with her head down. Isabella cannot see her face to measure her reaction. She believed she will ask her papa about her situation. She needed to quiet herself before her face became contorted also.

"Miss Linton, please distribute these wills to the family," asked Sir Linton.

"Right away, Sir Linton."

"Ladies and gentlemen, we have come to the conclusion of our reading. I implore you to not argue this will as per your mother's desire. Miss Linton, please escort the ladies to the great hall. I desire that you, Robert and Edward, remain with me for a moment.

"Gentlemen, your mother desires I give you each a letter. Miss Linton will be giving Fanny a letter as well. Thank you for your time, gentlemen. Oh, Robert, you and John both need to set up an interview with me by end of week," requested Sir Linton.

"Is there a problem, Sir Linton?" asked John Dashwood.

"I am not at liberty to discuss anything at this moment, gentlemen."

"Ladies," said Miss Linton. "Please have a sit down while Sir Linton is with the gentlemen. Mrs. Dashwood, here is a letter for you from your mother. Is everything all right, Mrs. Dashwood?" asked Miss Linton.

"Why yes, of course, Miss Linton. This letter is a bit of a surprise. Thank you, Miss Linton," said Fanny.

"Forgive me, Miss Linton, but is Sir Linton not your father?" asked Lucy.

"Yes, Mrs. Ferrars, Sir Linton is my father, but we have an understanding when business is in session."

"I have never heard of ladies being involved in business. It is not customary," bellowed Lucy.

"Oh, Mrs. Ferrars, it is very customary here at Linton Park," replied Isabella with an authoritative voice. "My father, Sir Linton, is much involved in my future endeavors. That is one of many factors that makes him a wonderful father."

"Miss Linton, I hope you don't find me impertinent, but you look very familiar to me. Have we met before elsewhere?" asked Lucy.

"No, Mrs. Ferrars, I am quite certain our paths have never crossed. I would surely have remembered you."

Isabella noticed Lucy bearing a quizzical brow after her response. Their discussion came to an end after that exchange. As she walked away, she overheard Lucy whispering to Fanny that she must try to remember where she has seen Isabella before. She then heard Fanny telling Lucy to hush. As she continued to walk to her papa's office, she noticed Elinor in the reflection of her papa's glass door smiling as Fanny told Lucy to hush. She could not help herself but to stop and turn around to speak to Elinor.

"Ms. Elinor, how are Kennedi and Brody doing?"

"They are doing well, Isabella, thank you for asking," replied Elinor.

"I have plans to see them very soon. I desire for us all to go riding. I believe I shall ride Thunder to your house. We must also invite Abel and Addison along with their horses. Please give them my best."

"Yes, Isabella," replied Elinor. "They are excited for your next visit. I shall make them aware of your impending visit with Thunder."

Fanny asked Elinor, "How are you to keep the horses that my mother generously bequeathed your son and Edward?"

"It is a generous gift that was given by your mother. Edward and Brody will be much appreciative for these gifts. As far as a place for keeping the horses, it will not be a problem. We already have stables for the horses that we have," replied Elinor.

"Oh, I did not realize that a parson could afford such luxuries," said Fanny.

"It was a gift from your mother on her last visit to us," replied Elinor.

"My mother visited you?" asked Fanny.

"Yes, Fanny," said Elinor. "She took great pleasure in joining us at our parsonage a few times."

"I see! Please relate my best to your children," said Fanny.

"Thank you, Fanny. I shall."

Elinor thought it would be impertinent if she did not inquire about Lucy and Robert. Before Elinor could inquire about Lucy and Robert, Lucy interrupted Elinor by asking how the small church was coming along. Elinor understood Lucy's question to be a condescending one.

"My dear Lucy, our church has long ago been small. Edward's sermons over the years has created great interest in our church. We have tripled our worshippers as well as the size of the parsonage. Our family has been very blessed, and we give God all the glory," replied Elinor.

"Amen!" said Isabella. "Papa and I truly enjoy listening to Parson Edward."

"Well, Elinor," replied Lucy. "God has certainly blessed you extra today with all the surprising gifts that Edward has received from his mother's will."

"Indeed, Lucy," replied Elinor. We remember when you decided to marry Robert after Mrs. Ferrars disinherited Edward for his engagement to you. That inheritance was a great blessing also, was it not? Nothing else to say, Lucy? Ladies, if you will excuse me, I must get some fresh air. I will wait for Edward in our barouche."

I am very pleased to see that Elinor finally stood up for herself, thought Isabella.

As Elinor stepped away, Lucy's mouth dropped open, and her face became red. Fanny stood up and demanded Lucy to keep her reserve.

"Did you think that Elinor was the only person who is aware of your deceit and manipulation? After all, Lucy, Elinor spoke the truth. There might have been a slight amount of delight in her conduct, but nonetheless, Elinor spoke the truth!" said Fanny.

Nothing but silence surrounded Fanny and Lucy in the great hall as they waited for their husbands. As the reading had ended, all the families departed in silence.

Isabella and her papa watched in amazement as there were not any pleasantries save one. Edward extended his hand out to his brother Robert and John Dashwood.

"Do you see, Isabella? Nothing has changed for the better. I believe that Mrs. Ferrars's will might have made it worse."

"Yes, Papa, I believe you are in earnest."

"Isabella, I am certain that Evelynn Ferrars was trying to change her situation with her children. She may have even learned by watching her son Edward and his family on her visits this past year."

"Oh, how I wish that to be true, Papa. Everyone deserves to be happy."

"Miss Linton, Robert Ferrars and John Dashwood will set up their interviews with me soon. I will need their reports from the vault so I may continue to work on them."

"Yes, Sir Linton, as you wish. Oh, by the way, Lucy was inquiring in a condescending manner as to why I should be involved with your business."

"What was your response, dearest?"

"I replied that you and I have an understanding for my future and that this is how things are conducted at Linton Park."

"That is the true response, dearest. There is no need for any more information on our personal situation."

"Thank you, Papa."

3

John and Fanny Dashwood

"John, have you made your interview with Sir Linton?" asked Fanny.

"Yes, Fanny. I am to go this morning."

"John, what is it that he wants with you?"

"I do not know, Fanny, but I will take care of any situation should it arise."

"Very well, John," answered Fanny.

After John left for his interview with Sir Linton, Fanny went into the sitting room to have a sit down with her letter from her mother.

Fanny sat on the davenport, looking down at the unopened letter. She tried to imagine what could possibly be said by her mother that was not passed down while she lived. Why was it so important to her mother to write this letter rather than have a discussion with her when she was alive? Thirty minutes had passed since she sat down. Finally, she reached for the letter opener and began to open the letter.

My Dearest Fanny,

I am writing this letter because I have not the courage to say my thoughts to you intimately. I feel that I have done my best to prepare you for the world. I have ensured your place in the first circle and guided you to a place of higher rank.

You have indeed fulfilled your destiny as far as social standing. I feel I did my duty by you.

Where I have failed is in giving you the nurturing you should have received. Your father was a wonderful loving man who knew how to show affection. If not for his death, I believe you and Robert would have benefitted from him. I raised you with all that I knew. If I am to be honest, affection was not part of our understanding.

Your brother Edward received the full benefit from your father.

I have learned, late in my life, that being in the first circle pales in comparison to affection. The warmth and tenderness that comes out of affection is a wonderful thing.

I ask one thing from you. Let yourself be loved and love those most cherished around you that seek nothing but love in return.

Your brother Edward and his family, have a wonderful understanding of affection. It would be in your best interest to appraise their situation and learn from them.

It is not too late, dearest. I desire you much love and am sorry for falling short. Please forgive me Fanny. Turn right your wrongs against others if possible before it is too late.

All my love,
Your mother

Fanny sat quietly, looking over the letter again and again. Mother, how could you dismiss such a basic foundation as affection? Searching her mind, she finds no answer but is now in a state of aggrievement. She must compose herself so that John would not see her in this state of mind.

Tea, she thought. *I must have tea.*

John Dashwood finally arrived at Linton Park for his required interview.

"Good morning, Miss Linton. I am here for my interview with Sir Linton."

"Good morning, Mr. Dashwood. Please come in and settle yourself in Sir Linton's office. May I get you a cup of tea?"

"Yes please."

When Isabella returned to the office with Mr. Dashwood's tea, she noticed him sitting quietly with a perplexed look on his face. "Here is your tea, Mr. Dashwood."

"Thank you, Miss Linton."

She went to stand behind her papa's desk on the right side and waited for his arrival.

Sir Linton walked in and extended pleasantries with Mr. Dashwood.

"Mr. Dashwood," said Sir Linton. "I have been you and your family's barrister for many years as was my father. You and I have a lawful and financial arrangement. Miss Linton will serve as my assistant and observer during our interview today. Very well, let us carry on. Mr. Dashwood, you are here in regard to your finances. It has come to my attention that your finances have decreased greatly. Your properties are also in arrears."

Isabella stood silent and watched Mr. Dashwood's every movement and state of discomfort. She had not ever been privy to anyone's financial situation. *Here sits this man having been in the first circle for decades and now in danger of great financial loss,* thought Isabella.

"I don't comprehend what you mean, Sir Linton," said Mr. Dashwood.

"John, I cannot believe that your financial status has been diminished without your understanding," remarked Sir Linton.

Mr. Dashwood sat in silence with a frightened look upon his face.

"John," spoke Sir Linton. "Your home in London and Norland are in arrears. They are currently being reclaimed by the bank. I have documents from the bank saying that you were sent several notices about this situation. There are also several emporiums that have interviewed with me in regard to high credit balances. They also have copies of letters they have sent you. All these items are irrefutable, John. What is going on?" asked Sir Linton.

Mr. Dashwood sat in a slumping position with a look of horror.

"Sir Linton, apparently I have not assessed my financial situation. If I were to release the Norland home, could we remain in our London home?"

"John, you do not understand the severity of your present situation," replied Sir Linton. "You will not be able to afford either house. It requires a great amount of funds to maintain either. You must now concentrate on final payments to all the emporiums, ornament houses, and haberdasheries. You do not want to end up in debtor's prison."

"How could I have let this happen?" said Mr. Dashwood.

Isabella felt sorry for Mr. Dashwood, but as her papa had always told me, one makes or breaks themselves.

"John, this is not all your doing. Fanny also bears great responsibility. Fanny has an exorbitant appetite for the finest as well as maintaining her status in the first circle."

"What is my recourse, Sir Linton?" asked John.

"My suggestion is to immediately put on the market both houses and find a much smaller house with less land and servants. I have profiled for you and Fanny a step-by-step course of action which will work if you follow my advice. When you have regained command of your estate, your total fund will afford you two thousand pounds per month. That amount is a total for home, servants, and anything else you desire. It is imperative that you immediately commence this course of action."

Isabella thought Mr. Dashwood was going to faint where he stood.

"What am I going to tell Fanny? This is the only life she has known and excelled at. She knows of nothing else," said John with much concern.

"John," said Sir Linton. "Tell Fanny the truth. It is the best course. I am sorry for your current situation, but you and Fanny must adjust. There is no other alternative. I must also make you aware of a four-month time limit in which to get your situation in order. I have written out a plan of execution which will help you to follow the plan."

"Thank you, Sir Linton and Miss Linton, for working on our behalf," said John.

"Miss Linton," asked Sir Linton. "Will you please verify these documents and be sure to give Mr. Dashwood his set?"

"Yes, Sir Linton, immediately."

Isabella watched her father escort Mr. Dashwood through the great hall and then outdoors. She began to realize why her papa wanted her to comprehend his business. *Papa desires me to learn how to be a self-reliant female within current and future situations.*

"Papa, what do you believe will come about with John and Fanny?"

"Well, dearest, the situation is that Fanny has always been of a single thought. She believes that all that is of importance is her standing in the first circle and all that comes with. It will be a great difficult situation in the Dashwood home."

"I agree, Papa. One must have stability in life."

* * * * *

John finally arrived at Norland Park only to remain in the barouche to prepare himself for relating the distressing revelation to Fanny.

Fanny heard the trollop of the horses and stood up to see who it was. As she looked out, she saw that it was John, but why did he remain in the barouche?

John saw Fanny through the window and finally decided to enter the house and get to it.

John guided Fanny into the parlor for their conversation.

They have not been seated when Fanny asked him of his interview with Sir Linton.

"John, did Sir Linton speak of an error in my mother's will?"

"No, my dear, that matter is long settled and closed."

"What is it then, John? What are you to tell me?"

"My dear, please let us sit down."

"I have been sitting long enough, waiting for you to return. I feel I must stand, John."

"Fanny, I must tell you about our grave situation."

"What do you mean grave situation? We have not a grave situation. Our situation is well preserved."

"Fanny, please listen to me for once." John noticed Fanny's lips getting tight and her eyes glaring.

"Oh, for heaven's sake, John, out with it."

John stood upright as possible and released the words that had haunted him during his journey home from Linton Park: "Fanny, we are in financial ruin. Did you hear what I said?"

All of a sudden, Fanny's legs left her as she plopped down onto the davenport left to them by her mother.

"Dearest," asked John. "Are you well?"

"No, John, I am not believing what you are saying. What kind of irrational talk is this? Why would you say this?"

"Fanny, I am in earnest. It is but too true."

"On what grounds are you telling me this? Where did you hear this, John?"

"I have been told by Sir Linton that we together, Fanny, have amassed great debt over many years. We can no longer retain what we have."

"No!" said Fanny. "That is a lie."

"My dear, Sir Linton has given me certified documentation that supports the discovery of our financial disaster."

"John, I have no desire to speak of this any further."

"Fanny, you cannot ignore this. You must attend to what I am telling you. We can no longer live the life within the first circle as we have for many years! Sir Linton said that we are to relinquish Norland as well as our house in London. The banks have started recovery against us for the houses."

"John, where are we to live? What are we to do? I cannot exist outside of our social standing."

"Fanny, we no longer have a social standing. We have not a choice, dearest. Sir Linton has given me a schedule for repayment to everyone that we have debt with. When all is finished, we will only have two thousand pounds per month total to live on."

"No, John, no! We cannot live with two thousand pounds a month. There must be more funds elsewhere."

"Fanny, it is so. We have nothing else to draw from. I have been shown the confirmation."

"This is all your doing, John! How can you let this happen?"

"Dearest, I will agree to take the majority of the accountability, but you are to accept your part in our situation."

No sound was heard as John and Fanny sat on the davenport, glaring down as to what seemed like hours.

"John, we are ruined. What will become of us? There will be whispers, and we will be found out. For shame, for shame! We will also lose our acquaintances who will no longer socialize with us."

"Dearest, if we are to lose our acquaintances, then I believe they were not true friends. We must accept and do the best we can. Many people live by smaller means all the time. My stepmother and sisters are a good example. Let us retire, my dear, for it has been a long day."

* * * * *

The next morning showed promise. The sun was beaming, the birds were chirping, and a more cordial atmosphere between John and Fanny.

Fanny asked John as to the sort of house they might have.

"Dearest, I have given this much thought. The house must be far from London and in the countryside. I remember traveling to Plymouth and stopping at Brookshire in Somerset at a house called Bratton Lodge to water the horses. The tenant, Mr. Earlie, was very kind and showed me the property. The house has three bedrooms and quarters for two servants. It also had a small stable and a lovely garden."

"John, this is very difficult for me to say. I could not sleep last night for thoughts of my past actions against others. Dearest, do you believe in reclamation?"

"Fanny, I never gave it a thought, but my father's words come back to me about taking care of my stepmother and sisters. We had so much and them so little. This indeed could be our reclamation, Fanny. I shall inquire as to who owns the Bratton Lodge and make an interview with them."

"John, this will mean starting all over again with very little."

"Yes, dearest. Maybe it is as it should be. There is one positive situation—we will be closer to our family if they will have us."

"John, do you think they will forgive us for how we treated them?"

"I have hope, my dear," replied John with a smile.

4

Robert and Lucy Ferrars

"Isabella, we have only one interview this morning, then we will have the afternoon at our leisure."

"That is wonderful, Papa."

"I believe I hear a carriage outside, Miss Linton."

"Yes, Sir Linton, that would be Mr. and Mrs. Ferrars arriving for their interview. Are you certain that you want Lucy Ferrars in the interview?"

"Most definitely, Miss Linton. Give me five minutes then show them to my office."

"Yes, Sir Linton."

"Miss Isabella, do not forget about your piano lesson this afternoon," said Miss Wall.

"Thank you for reminding me, Miss Wall. I won't. Oh, Miss Wall, could you please ask Cook to bring tea to Papa's office? Thank you."

"Yes, miss."

"Good morning, Mr. and Mrs. Ferrars."

"Good morning, Miss Linton," said both Mr. and Mrs. Ferrars.

"Please follow me to Sir Linton's office. Come in and have a seat."

"Thank you," answered Mr. Ferrars.

"Miss Linton, I have been thinking about our last discussion," said Lucy.

"Our last discussion," replied Isabella.

"You still look very familiar to me. You remind me of someone, but I still cannot place you," said Lucy.

"I am sorry, Mrs. Ferrars, but I cannot help you."

"Ahh, here is Sir Linton at last," said Robert.

Isabella took her place at her father's right side in hopes that they begin soon.

"Good morning, Mr. and Mrs. Ferrars. We shall now begin our interview. As your barrister, it is my duty to inform you that your finances are in dire distress. I have sent you several notices in regard to this situation. Robert, you and Lucy have just about exhausted your inheritance from your mother. Your exorbitant spending is the cause."

"That is not possible," bellowed Robert. "You must be mistaken."

"Robert," said Lucy. "What does this mean?"

"Robert, Lucy," said Sir Linton. "It means no longer can you afford all the things that you both surround yourself with."

"Sir Linton," asked Robert. "What proof do you have of this situation?"

"Robert, I have several certified documents showing your home in arrears, and your debtors are demanding restitution."

"Robert," said Lucy. "This cannot be possible. What have you done to us?"

"Me, Lucy, me!" said Robert. "You cannot guilt me for this situation. You have done your share of relinquishing my inheritance."

Sir Linton and Isabella looked upon them without any comment.

"If it were not for my inheritance, Lucy, we would not have married."

"Excuse me, Robert and Lucy, but this is not the time nor place for a disagreement. We must return to the solution for your financial situation," said Sir Linton.

Isabella was witness to her first couple's squabble. This did not make her feel comfortable.

"Robert," said Sir Linton. "I have set up a restitution schedule that must be followed. You will not be able to remain in your home in Plymouth, for the bank has taken hold of it."

"Our house, Sir Linton," hollered Lucy. "You cannot take our house!"

"Mrs. Ferrars, I am not the one taking back your home, the bank is due to it being in arrears. Mr. and Mrs. Ferrars," continued Sir Linton. "You must comprehend the gravity of your financial situation. Your excessive expenditures over the years has caused your situation. Your inheritance balance, after repayment to your debtors, will allow you one thousand five hundred pounds per month."

"Surely you jest!" said Robert.

"No, Mr. Ferrars, I am in earnest," said Sir Linton.

"Robert, do something!" hollered Lucy.

"Be quiet, Lucy. I've had it with you!" growled Robert.

"Mr. Ferrars," said Sir Linton. "I need your signature on these documents, then we shall be done with our interview."

I have never been so cheerful to have an interview done with, thought Isabella.

"Thank you, Mr. and Mrs. Ferrars. I expect all to be well with your situation," said Sir Linton.

Isabella and her papa looked out the window as Robert and Lucy walked to their barouche that was inherited from his mother.

"Look at them, Papa. They treat each other like strangers."

"Yes, dearest. Unfortunately, that marriage was in disrepair before their financial situation gave way. You see, Isabella, one cannot have a good understanding with manipulations and deceit between them."

"I understand, Papa. They seem to not have affection for each other."

"You are very observant, my dear, and that is a good quality to have."

* * * * *

There was nothing but silence between Robert and Lucy the whole way home. When they arrived home, they both went to the parlor to sit.

"I cannot believe you spoke up so loudly at the interview," said Robert. "Have you no decency?"

"Well, if you were more of a man, we might not be in this financial disaster. It was your responsibility to take heed of the finances, not mine!" said Lucy.

"It might have been my responsibility, but your continuous spending and desire to be in the first circle certainly did not help our situation, Lucy. I was better off when I was a bachelor with no responsibilities. Now I am expected to dwell with you and barely have funds to support what I desire."

"It is too late for all that now, Robert. You must find us a house we can afford."

"It must be a home in the countryside. We need to relieve ourselves from the first circle, Lucy."

"Robert, I have worked hard to obtain my standing."

"I know you have," said Robert sternly. "Do you not think I understand why you married me? You knew full well, as the rest of my family, that my mother was disinheriting Edward for agreeing to marry you. You manipulated your way into this marriage."

"Really, Robert? You are the one who proposed to me. I don't recall any ladies wanting your attention during that time."

"Well, Lucy, you got what you wanted from this pretense of a marriage. I have nothing else to give as we have nothing now. I believe I may ask Sir Linton to petition parliament for me a divorce," said Robert.

"Robert, you cannot be in earnest. We have had good times between us. It was not all bad. I cannot be divorced. It will make me shameful, and I have nowhere to go. Do you not believe we can be better now that we have spoken these words about each other?"

"Lucy, you are a conniving and manipulative woman. Those traits cannot change easily. You began acting like this before you encountered Elinor and thought about Edward having affection for her."

"I know what I have done, Robert. You need not bring into remembrance of that time. You are just as blameworthy of wrongdoings, my dear. Perhaps we do have something in common."

"Our reclamation is at hand, Lucy, do you not understand?"

"Reclamation for what, Robert?"

"For all the wrongdoings that we have done to others, Lucy."

"Why are you speaking of these things, Robert?"

"The letter from my mother made me realize my errors and the need for restitution in order to rectify my situation."

"And yet you threaten me with divorce, Robert."

"You are right, dearest. I must start with charity within my own house."

"What did you call me, Robert?"

"What do you mean, Lucy?"

"You just now referred to me as dearest. You have not used that word in many years."

"You are right, Lucy. I do miss those days of fawning at the start."

"Oh, Robert, can we truly start over and be happy with so little?"

"Dearest, it is the little things that matter and bloom into larger and better situations. It took my mother's letter to guide me to where we should go from here."

"I am in agreement, my dear," replied Lucy. "We together shall enter into this new journey with open hearts and restoration."

"I think on my brother Edward and have come to the conclusion that he got it right from the beginning."

"Let us retire, dearest, for tomorrow we start a new and better situation for ourselves."

"I am in agreement, dear," replied Lucy.

5

Edward and Elinor Ferrars

Since the beginning, Edward and Elinor were committed to each other. Neither rank nor status mattered. They were as dedicated to their family as they were to themselves with great affection.

Edward and Elinor, along with their children, Kennedi and Brody, resided at Delaford Parish, for Edward was the parson there. They were surrounded by family and many acquaintances. Elinor was the county's French teacher.

Edward's parish had flourished greatly over the years. He had what he had desired for many years. The family had much affection for each other and the peace of country living.

Edward was not treated well by his first family, but that did not change his disposition. Edward and Elinor had unknowingly set the example of love, marriage, and family for others, particularly his first family.

Country living had afforded the Ferrars family tranquility and abundance.

Their children, Kennedi and Brody, were in charge of the cows, goats, horses, and pigs. Edward had full charge of his beloved chickens.

The children were both much involved with their twin cousins, Abel and Addison, as well as Isabella Linton.

Both Edward and Elinor made for certain that Edward's forced social standards growing up never saw its way into his current family, for his desire was for the church, peace, and affection.

They frequently had gatherings after Edward's sermons with Elinor's first family. Edward's first family's status made no room for him, and he was content with that.

When Edward's mother, Mrs. Ferrars, died, he was given a letter from her. The letter spoke mostly of praise. She did, however, offer her apologies for her lack of nurturing. Edward realized, after reading her letter, that his mother did change for the better, and he was glad of it.

Edward always knew that his father was the reason for his disposition. He felt sorry for Robert and Fanny not being afforded the same opportunity. He also realized that there was not anything to be done to remedy their situation. He had not seen his sister or brother since their mother's funeral.

Elinor had always been close to her first family. She had always had an affectionate heart, but also carried herself with strength and comfort. She had been known to carry her first family even above her mother through difficulties with ease. Elinor was not one to show or share her feelings in front of anyone including her mother or sisters. Being the eldest, she took on responsibility with grace. That was one of the traits that Edward loved about her.

The parish had grown threefold since they arrived at Delaford.

Colonel Brandon, on more than one occasion, had said that Edward was the right man for the parish on his estate.

6

Colonel and Marianne Brandon

This was a story of affection that was born from heartache.

From the beginning, Colonel Brandon was in love with Marianne. He would do and did anything for her. The colonel observed Marianne as she went through moments of heartbreak and despair because of a man called John Willoughby. This man let go of Marianne because he wanted to marry a woman with money instead of love.

As Marianne suffered, so did Colonel Brandon.

In time, Marianne would understand what true affection was because of the colonel's patience and affection.

Providence brought Colonel Brandon and Marianne together, and now, affection kept them secure. They had both amassed many blessings. Their financial future was secure. They had two wonderful children—twins Abel and Addison—a large home, much land, and a wonderful relationship with their families.

Colonel Brandon had since retired himself from the Army.

Marianne joyfully filled her time with teaching students the pianoforte.

They resided at Delaford Estate in Dorsetshire.

Her sister, Elinor, and husband, along with their two children, resided at the parish at Delaford Estate.

The colonel and Marianne's twins, Abel and Addison, both sixteen, attended Allenham Academy. They were both excellent horse riders and spoke fluent French, thanks to their Aunt Elinor. The twins were very close to their cousins, Kennedi and Brody, as well as Isabella Linton, who Marianne taught the pianoforte.

Marianne had grown much since the days of that blaggard John Willoughby. He truly had left a scar upon her heart which had lovingly been healed by the colonel.

Abel and Addison were much loved by their parents.

Marianne had long ago taken a special enthusiasm for Isabella since the poor child lost her mother. Marianne, from the beginning, had had a curious attachment to Isabella and treated her like she was her own daughter. Marianne could not explain the cause for her attachment to Isabella as she continued to show her affection.

Colonel Brandon also had an attachment to Isabella and was called uncle by her due to his kind nature and close friendship with Sir Philip Linton.

There were many gatherings at Delaford which allowed for much affection between family and guests.

Marianne's sister, Margaret Dashwood, who was the geography teacher at Allenham Academy, and her mother, Mrs. Dashwood, were very much involved with the Brandons. They also carried much affection for Edward and Elinor's children, Kennedi and Brody. The children loved to visit their aunt Margaret and grandmother at Barton Cottage.

The once little cottage held many memories—favorable and not.

Margaret lived there with her mother and friend, Melanie Ozburn, who was the literature teacher at Allenham Academy.

Mrs. Dashwood had made several improvements to the cottage as promised years ago. It was now an even more charming cottage. Sir John Middleton, Mrs. Dashwood's cousin, had deeded her the cottage as well as ten thousand pounds from an early inheritance. He knew that John and Fanny Dashwood did wrong by Mrs. Dashwood and the Dashwood sisters those many years ago.

Mrs. Dashwood realized that Marianne and the colonel are truly blessed for all these years.

7

Longtime Acquaintances

Sir Linton and Colonel Brandon had been friends for many years. Their friendship started when they were young lads in the Army. As long as they remembered, they had helped each other throughout good and bad times.

Sir Linton decided early on to leave the Army in pursuit of a legal occupation. While Colonel Brandon remained in the Army for several years after, even though they may have separated, they still continued their friendship to this day with a deeper appreciation for each other.

The colonel kissed Marianne farewell as he went for his weekly outing to Sir Linton's house on this fine sunny day.

As he galloped up to the house, he noticed that Isabella was outdoors, waiting for Thunder, her horse, to be brought to her.

"Good morning, dearest Isabella," said the colonel as he dismounted.

Isabella ran to him for an embrace. "Uncle, so good to see you again. I have missed you."

"And I you, Isabella."

"Where is Abel, uncle? I thought he was coming for our weekly ride?"

"Patience, my dear, for here he comes over the hill. You know he would not miss riding with you for anything."

"Ahh, I see him now. Are you and papa looking forward to your weekly get-together?"

"Of course, Isabella. Your papa and I have much to discuss which includes your upcoming birthday ball."

"Uncle, I am so excited for my ball. Papa had made for me the most beautiful dress."

"I shall be excited to see you wearing it, dearest," answered the colonel.

"Well, here is Abel finally. We must be off. Will I see you later, uncle?"

"Most assuredly, dearest. Abel, be sure to watch out for Isabella and yourself. Do not ride too far off."

"Yes, Papa, we won't ride too far," answered Abel. "Are you now ready, Miss Isabella?" asked Abel.

"Why, yes, Mr. Brandon, I am. Oh, uncle, go on in. I believe Papa is setting up for your visit in his office."

"On my way in," said the colonel.

"Oh, Philip, where are you, old chum?" called the colonel.

"Here, old chap, in my office. Do come in and have a sit down. I have prepared the brandy and cigars. I have also gotten Cook to make us some sweet cakes for our visit."

"Why thank you, Philip, just don't tell Marianne about me eating these sweet cakes."

They both laughed as they thought of Marianne scolding the colonel for eating the sweet cakes.

"Philip, I do have a bit of business to discuss with you."

"Yes, what is it?"

"I would like for you to draw up a contract of deed of transference for me."

"Of course I will, Chris. Who is the party to be involved in this transaction?"

"I want Edward and Elinor Ferrars to be given the parish, the parsonage, and 150 acres that surround it, which has already been surveyed. Here are the papers."

"Chris, that is a very generous offering. You have always been a kind and generous man. Have you spoken to them about this gift yet?"

"No, I plan on telling them after the church picnic on Sunday next. They have worked so hard on that land and with the parish that I felt it time to reward all their efforts."

"I shall draw the papers up myself tomorrow and have my man Jonesy hand deliver it to you."

"Thank you, Philip. Send me the bill along with the papers."

"No need of payment, Christopher. I believe one good turn deserves another. Since it is for Edward and Elinor, it would be my pleasure. I am very fond of them both."

"Thank you, Philip, that is very generous of you."

"You are most welcome, my old friend," said Sir Linton.

"Philip, how are we coming along with our Isabella's birthday ball?"

"Well, I have enlisted Miss Wall's help along with Cook."

"Excellent notion, Philip. Us old men need all the help possible."

"I am in agreement," said Sir Linton.

"The food has been placed on order. The ornaments are being taken care of by Miss Wall, and the cake has been preordered and am glad of it," said Philip.

"Sounds as if you have everything just so. I was told by Isabella that you had her dress commissioned by the finest clothier."

"Yes, sir, I have. Isabella told me of her desired colors, and the rest is coming along."

"You and I know, Philip, that nothing is too good for our girl. You have done a wonderful thing raising her."

"Thank you, Chris. My wife and I, before she died, had many discussions on how Isabella should be raised. I just desire that she would be with us today to see our lovely Isabella."

"I do also, Philip. She was a wonderful woman and is missed greatly."

"Philip, about Isabella, how are we to approach the letter from her mother and when?"

"Well, Chris, I believe we should present the letter to her a few days after her birthday. I don't want anything to disturb her elation."

"I agree, Philip. This letter could cause her distress with the information contained."

"Chris, we have to approach this situation with great caution."

"What do you mean, Philip?"

"It has been brought to my understanding twice, by Isabella, that Lucy Ferrars is trying to make out who Isabella reminds her of."

"Lucy is not the only one, my friend. Marianne, for years, has had an unusual attachment with Isabella—which, by all means, is not a bad thing—but there is a stirring in her about Isabella that she cannot account for. I have not examined this stirring for the sake of my wife."

"I see. Chris, we have only been concerned about Isabella and not thought of the others involved."

"Philip, our first concern must be for Isabella and desire that love will ease this situation for the rest. We have made sure that Isabella has not ever surrounded herself with this problem. She has never made mention of any problem and is still unaware, for now, of this situation."

"Well, Chris, I am glad of that, for she has always been surrounded by people who love her and would see no harm befall her."

"Yes, and a great example of this would be my son Abel. I believe they have a special attachment."

"I am in agreement, Chris. I could not have chosen a better fellow than Abel for Isabella."

8

Allenham Academy

Allenham Academy was a fairly new school. It was a gift through Lady Allen's will after her passing. Sir Linton had been put in place to be the barrister for the academy as well as chairman in charge, as per Lady Allen's request.

Mrs. Wilson had been put in place as head mistress. The talented staff included Miss Margaret Dashwood as the geography instructor; Miss Melanie Ozburn, the literature instructor; Mrs. Crouch, the mathematics instructor; Mr. Chesterfield, the science instructor; and Mrs. Watson, the pianoforte instructor. All these instructors were appraised and highly qualified.

Great performances were expected from all the students. Strict adherence to rules and regulations was demanded despite being a progressive academy.

The students had returned from spring holiday and seemed eager to get to business.

Miss Dashwood, the geography instructor, asked the students to be seated as they walked in. Millicent Willoughby pushed by Isabella to attain a seat next to Abel Brandon, much to his dislike.

Miss Dashwood called roll:

1. Constance Asbury
2. Abel Brandon
3. Addison Brandon

4. Henry Cunningham
5. Brody Ferrars
6. Kennedi Ferrars
7. Ashley Harns
8. Isabella Linton
9. William Pringle
10. John Taylor
11. Andrew Thomas
12. Millicent Willoughby

"Good morning, students."

"Good morning, Miss Dashwood," was said by all.

"Good to see you, ladies and gentlemen. I hope you all had a wonderful holiday. Please take out your paper tablets, pencil, and geography book."

Abel leaned back in his seat and tried to take a glance at Isabella.

"Mr. Brandon, is there a problem with your desk?" asked Miss Dashwood.

"No, Miss Dashwood, just stretching a bit."

Isabella had a smile on her face for she knew exactly what Abel was doing. *He would not need to do that if Millie did not rush to sit in my chair*, thought Isabella.

Miss Dashwood also knew what was happening as she noticed Kennedi and Brody smiling.

Addison just shook her head because she knew what Millie was doing concerning her brother Abel.

"Ladies and gentlemen, please turn to page 89. We are going to be discussing why the Nile River is so important to the indigenous tribes. Please read carefully so we may have a discussion on my question. As you read, you need to write down anything of importance. As a separate task, you will be in charge of an investigation of history of any home of your choosing."

As class moved forward, all the students finished their assignment.

The students were walking to their next class when Millie stepped in front of Isabella, which made the rest of the students curious.

What is it, Millie?" asked Isabella.

I was thinking about our geography class and wondered how you felt about being an orphan like the children in the tribe?

Abel quickly stepped in front of Millie and reprimanded her in front of everyone. Kennedi, Brody, and Addison also spoke up.

"It is all right, everyone," said Isabella. "I will answer your impertinent question. Being an orphan made me sad, but knowing that I was especially chosen by my father, Sir Linton, is a great honor. Do you have any other questions, Millie?" asked Isabella.

Millie stood there silently as the group rebuffed her, except for Isabella, and then all walked away.

"My friends," said Isabella. "Do not worry about me, for I can take care of myself. I do, however, appreciate your concern."

"You know she is jealous of you," said Kennedi. "She is also enchanted with Abel."

"Yes, dearest, I am well aware of her fondness for Abel."

"Isabella, you must know that Abel does not care for her," said Addison.

"I am well aware of how Abel feels about Millie," said Isabella. "There is something wanting in her, but I cannot reason what it is."

"I don't think she is fetching," replied Brody.

"Well," said Isabella. "I cannot concern myself with her conduct at the moment. Let us go to math class before Mrs. Crouch starts looking for us."

* * * * *

As Isabella was sitting in math class, her thoughts began to wonder—who were her parents and what were they like. *I have never spoken to Papa about this because he is a wonderful father and Mum a wonderful mother before she died.* The word *orphan* brought a notion of loneliness and despair.

"Isabella, Isabella!" said Mrs. Crouch.

Isabella finally came out of her private thoughts. "Yes, Mrs. Crouch."

"Are you with us today?' asked Mrs. Crouch.

"Yes, please forgive me. I was much in thought."

"Very well, tell me the response to problem 9," said Mrs. Crouch.

"Negative twelve," answered Isabella.

"Very good, Isabella," replied Mrs. Crouch.

Abel leaned over and asked Isabella if she was all right.

"All is well, Mr. Brandon. I shall keep my wit about me."

Addison noticed Millie giving Isabella a sour look as she was responding to Abel's inquiry.

"Class," said Mrs. Crouch. "We will have a mathematics exam on Monday next. Please be sure to evaluate your notes and work at home so that you may do well."

Math class was over, and it was lunchtime. The whole group strolled into the dining hall and sat down.

"I am so hungry I could eat a horse," bellowed Brody.

"Well, it best be your horse you eat because I need mine to ride home on," replied Abel.

Everyone began to laugh until the instructors looked on.

As they were finishing their lunch, Isabella asked, "Do you ever wonder who lived here at Allenham before it became our school?"

"You may ask any of our parents, for they would know," said Abel.

"Know what, Mr. Brandon?" asked Miss Ozburn.

"We were pondering on who lived here before it was made our academy," repeated Isabella.

"Oh, that is an easy answer to find," replied Miss Ozburn. "We shall ask Miss Dashwood, for she has lived here for many years and knows everyone."

"Wonderful," said Isabella. "I shall ask her."

* * * * *

"Miss Dashwood."

"Yes, Isabella."

"I have an interest in doing my assignment on Allenham Academy and wish to discover who lived here before it became our school."

"Oh, Miss Isabella, that is an easy question. It was Lady Allen."

"I have never heard of her," replied Isabella.

"Lady Allen would also have other family members live here for part of the year. She had a favorite nephew who spent much time here. As it happens, her nephew's daughter studies at this academy."

"A daughter?" said Isabella.

"Yes, dear. You know of her. Her name is Millicent Willoughby."

"Millie! Surely you jest, Miss Dashwood."

"No, I am in earnest," replied Miss Dashwood. "I do not know if Miss Millie knows of Allenham history, but her father knows very much. Her father, Mr. Willoughby, comes by often to get his daughter out of school early so that they get Millie home to her governess as they attend many gatherings in the first circle."

"That story gives me grief and might explain her behavior, Miss Dashwood."

"That is a very astute observation, Miss Isabella."

"Miss Linton?" called Mrs. Wilson.

"Yes, Mrs. Wilson, you called."

"Is your job this week not to be the door monitor?"

"Yes, Mrs. Wilson. I will get right to it."

* * * * *

Abel and Brody hollered Isabella's name from down the hall.

"Shush, gentlemen, for you will get us in trouble."

There was a loud knock at the front door, which made Isabella jump back.

"Look through the peephole first!" yelled Abel.

"I am!" yelled Isabella. "Yes, sir, to whom am I speaking to?"

"My name is John Willoughby and am here to get my daughter Millicent."

"Please come in, Mr. Willoughby, and have a sit down."

"Thank you, miss," said Willoughby. "I have not seen you before."

"No, sir, we have never met. My name is Isabella Linton."

"Ahh, are you, by any chance, Sir Linton's daughter?"

"Yes, sir, I am."

As Isabella moved closer to the front desk, she felt as if Mr. Willoughby was studying her.

Where have I seen this child before? thought Willoughby. *She looks very familiar—her large black eyes dark as night, hair the color of molasses, rosy cheeks, and full lips. Pretty little thing.*

"Papa, I am here," hollered Millie.

"Ahh, Millie are you ready to go?"

Millie was being overly sweet because she knew Isabella was watching. "Yes, Papa. Will you be taking me dress shopping?"

"No, Millie, your mother and I are going out this evening."

"Again! When will I get to go also?"

Isabella stood by the desk with her back turned to Mr. Willoughby and Millie but could still hear all.

"Miss Linton, it was a great pleasure to meet you and hope to meet again."

"Thank you, sir. Goodbye, Millie, see you tomorrow."

Millie did not respond and was soon scolded by her father.

Why should he want to meet me again? she wondered. On further examination, Isabella thought she knew why Millie behaved the way she did. It seemed that this Mr. Willoughby and her mother did not want time with their daughter. *I am so fortunate to have a papa that loves me and spends time with me.*

Their last class was to be with Miss Ozburn. The ladies loved their poetry reading, but the boys not so much.

It is now time to go home. I must first check the door.

"Woohoo?" shouted Abel.

"Mr. Brandon, you frightened me, you rascal!"

"That is what will happen when you turn your back to doors. Now, let us get our horses and ride home," said Abel.

"I do not believe I want to ride alongside of you, Mr. Brandon."

"All right, all right. I apologize for frightening you. Now let us ride home."

"Very well then."

9

John Willoughby

All the way home, the sun was shining, and a nice breeze blew about their faces. Abel did not know that Isabella had an attachment for him, but she was not ready to admit it.

As they arrived at Delaford, she spoke to Abel about wanting to know more about Mr. Willoughby.

"Why should you want to know more about him?" asked Abel.

"For Allenham history's sake and because he seems very interesting."

"Leave old man Willoughby alone. He is dry as toast," said Abel.

At that moment, the colonel came out to see all the commotion. "What are you two doing?"

"We were speaking on our geography assignment," said Isabella. "I believe I will do mine on Allenham Academy history."

"Abel," asked the colonel. "What will your report be on?"

"I don't know at the moment, Papa. It is not fair that Miss Isabella just met someone from Allenham's history," said Abel.

"Oh," said the colonel. "Who can that possibly be, dearest?"

"A man by the name of John Willoughby."

"What!" The colonel's face became pale.

"Uncle, are you well? What is wrong?"

"Nothing, Isabella. I just remembered an interview that I am late for."

"Very well, uncle. I must be on my way home. See you tomorrow, Mr. Brandon." Isabella smiled.

"Until tomorrow." Abel waved.

"Abel," said the colonel. "You must not mention the name of John Willoughby in our home. Do you understand?"

"Yes, Papa, I will do as you ask. Is he dangerous? Who is this man?"

"I cannot discuss this with you right now. Please go inside and see if your mother is in need of anything."

Abel went inside and stood in the great hall. As he heard his mother playing the pianoforte, he wondered about Mr. Willoughby. *What could he have possibly done to warrant so much caution.*

His main concern now must be Isabella. He knew that she would not let this situation rest. He must discuss this further with her. He must warn her about his papa's request not to mention his name in our house.

* * * * *

Colonel Brandon's discovery of Willoughby led him straight to Sir Linton's front door.

"I will get the door, Papa. Uncle, what brings you here?"

"I forgot that I had an interview with your father."

"Aha, please come in. I will let Papa know that you are here."

"Thank you, dearest," said the colonel.

"Chris, were we to get together today?"

"No, Philip, but we need to talk. It is urgent."

"Please come into my office and close the door."

Isabella was headed back to her room when she noticed the door to her father's office was closed. *What is going on in there?* wondered Isabella. *I have never known Papa and uncle to be so mysterious.*

"Philip, Isabella met John Willoughby today!"

"What—where!"

"He came to get his daughter at the academy, and he spoke with her."

"I did not know he had a child at the academy," said Philip. "Oh, my, my, my."

"Apparently they were given an assignment by Miss Dashwood to search out the history of any place in England, and Isabella chose Allenham Academy, discovering that Willoughby resided there, if only temporarily, every year until Lady Allen dismissed him from the house."

"Here is what we will do, Chris. We gather both Isabella and Abel and tell them of Willoughby except for the outcome. They must be told because we know how they are. They will not let this rest until we have given a good reason. We must say it is for the sake of Marianne, which is not far from the truth, and they will respect that."

Chris listened very carefully and was in full agreement with his close chum Philip.

"Philip, we need to do this as soon as possible. May I bring Abel here after school tomorrow—if you are agreeable, of course."

"Agreed," answered Philip.

"I must be on my way now, Philip. We shall see you both tomorrow."

* * * * *

Today must be a good day, thought the colonel as he waited impatiently for his son Abel to arrive from school. He heard Marianne coming down the stairs and felt that he must calm himself for her sake.

"What is on your mind, dearest?" asked Marianne.

"What do you mean, my love?"

"Chris, you forget I know you and can tell if you are out of sort."

"Just business, dearest. Oh, Abel and I have an interview with Philip this afternoon."

"With Philip? Ahh, yes. I have forgotten that Abel is to continue his apprenticeship. When will he start his practicum this time?"

"That will be part of our discussion today, my dear wife."

"Very well, dearest. I will be much occupied, for I have two interviews for the pianoforte this afternoon. Here is our son now, Chris. Abel, you are to go to Sir Linton's today with your papa for a discussion on your practicum. Dearest, please give Isabella my love."

"Really, Papa," said Abel. "This is very exciting. Let me run and tell Benson not to unsaddle my horse."

"Ask Benson to saddle my horse, Abel, so that we may be off. Marianne, where is Addison?"

"She is upstairs in her room, tending to her classwork."

"Give her a kiss from her papa since I have not seen her."

"I shall, dearest. You and Abel ride cautiously."

"Papa!" shouted Abel. "We are ready!"

The colonel hugged and kissed Marianne before leaving the house. Marianne just smiled and waved goodbye as she thought to herself how blessed she is. The colonel said nothing to his son about the interview as they rode to Sir Linton's house.

When they arrived, Isabella was in the garden with Miss Wall, cutting fresh flowers for her papa's office. Isabella rose quickly when she saw her uncle and Abel ride up.

"Uncle, Abel, what are you doing here?"

"Good afternoon, dearest," said the colonel.

"Good afternoon, my fair lady," said Abel.

"Really, Abel, must you be so poetic?"

"But of course, I must."

Isabella blushed as she quickly showed them to the door. "Come in," said Isabella.

Sir Linton came out of his office to announce their interview.

"Papa, I did not know that we were conducting business this afternoon."

"Isabella," said Sir Linton. "Please join us in my office, for this interview requires explanation."

Isabella looked confused, but she did as her papa asked.

Everyone was seated when the colonel began his discussion.

"Isabella, Abel, you are both here so that as your papas, we can explain to you both why it is so important that the name of John

Willoughby must not be brought up. This interview is to remain between us four. Do you both understand what I am saying?"

Both Isabella and Abel replied yes as they looked at each other with frightened faces.

The colonel gathered his breath and said that he is going to tell them a story that is too true due to the fact that he was there when all this took place.

"Many years ago, when your mama, Abel, was young, she desperately fell in love with John Willoughby and he with her. He met her on one of his visits with his aunt, Lady Allen, in a place called Allenham. I was also in love with your mama, but she did not desire an attachment for me.

"Twenty years prior, I was in love with a woman called Eliza. My father sent me to the Army and her away from our house so that we could not be together due to her being poor. During that time apart, Eliza was with child out of wedlock from a man who abandoned them. Eliza had the baby and begged me to care for her because she was sick and dying. Out of guilt, I made sure Beth—was her name—lived with a caring family.

"Beth ran away and met a man by the name of John Willoughby, who when he found out she was with child, left her alone without telling her where he was going. This blaggard abandoned them both full well knowing of the shame and despair that Beth would have to go through. When he was found out by Lady Allen, his aunt, she sent him away and disowned him. That same day that Lady Allen found him out, he went to see Marianne and told her a lie as to why he must leave Devonshire.

"Your mama was devastated, Abel. Your mama did not see him till weeks later, at a gathering in London, she saw him with another lady. He had dismissed your mother all because he found a lady who had money and status who would bail him out. This whole situation hurt your mama and has taken many years to resolve itself. This is the reason why I don't want that man or his name mentioned."

Isabella and Abel sat there, astonished at the particulars in this story.

"Children, do you now comprehend the gravity of this situation?" asked the colonel.

"Papa," asked Abel. "What happened to Miss Beth?"

Sir Linton stood up quickly from his seat only to say that she went to live with acquaintances in the country to hide her situation.

"She has since passed on many years ago," said the colonel. "I understand that this is a heavy burden to carry, but it must be kept among us only. Can we make an agreement to continue to protect your mama, Abel, as well as your aunt, Isabella?"

Both Isabella and Abel agreed to the secret and not to speak of this to anyone else.

"Very well," said Sir Linton. "Let us have some refreshment before you and your papa depart."

"Oh, that sounds wonderful, Papa."

"By the way, Mr. Brandon, will you surely come to me in June and continue your apprenticeship?" asked Sir Linton.

"Most definitely," answered Abel. "I am very excited to continue to learn under the best law mind ever."

"There you go, Philip, high praise from your apprentice, my son."

"All right, everyone, let us get to the dining room for the refreshments."

10

Delaford Parish Picnic

"Now that our service has concluded," said Parson Ferrars. "Let us gather our goods and go outdoors for our picnic."

As everyone was gathering their goods, Isabella took a quick step toward Abel. "Abel," whispered Isabella. "We need to have a discussion about our secret. It must be away from others so they cannot hear."

"Why, of course. Come and find me later, and we shall walk to the covered bridge."

The families were all settled with their quilts under the massive oak tree which provided much needed shade.

Kennedi decided she would bring her floral quilt to share with Addison and Isabella.

"Addison, do you imagine that Andrew will come and sit with you?"

"I do not know. He is here, but he will have to search me out."

The ladies started giggling.

All of a sudden, a fish on a line dangled in front of Kennedi.

She screamed while the culprit, her brother Brody, was laughing very hard.

"Mr. Brody," spoke Miss Ginger, Kennedi's governess. "Please remove that fish at once!"

"Sorry, Miss Ginger."

"I am not the person who you should be apologizing to."

46

"Sorry, Kennedi, I was just having fun."

"Well, I thank you to take your fun elsewhere. Go play with the other boys."

"Dearest, who is that coming in the carriage?" asked Elinor.

"Why, that looks like Sir John and Mrs. Jennings, my dear."

"Oh, how wonderful. I was hoping they would join us."

"Hello, Edward. Hello, Elinor," said Mrs. Jennings.

"Sir John, Mrs. Jennings, how wonderful it is to see you both. Please come sit and partake with us," said Elinor.

"We would not have missed this for the world. Where is your dear mama, Mrs. Ferrars?"

"She is sitting with Marianne, the colonel, Margaret, and Miss Ozburn."

"How lovely it is to see everyone. Where are Kennedi and Brody, Mrs. Ferrars?"

"Kennedi has brought her own quilt and is sharing it with Addison and Isabella. Brody is at the brook, fishing with the boys."

"You both have such a beautiful daughter and handsome son," said Mrs. Jennings.

"Thank you so much, Mrs. Jennings."

"Edward, may I have a word with you?" asked Sir John.

"Of course. Let us go walk to the table."

* * * * *

"What can I do for you, Sir John?"

"Well, it is a peculiar situation, Edward, involving your sister and her husband, John."

"Peculiar situation, Sir John."

"They are renting the Bratton house from me in Brookshire."

"I don't understand, Sir John. Why do they need to rent a home for they have a house in London and a country house in Sussex?"

"I was told through a barrister friend of mine in Somersetshire that they have lost their houses and fortune and cannot afford their former lives within the first circle."

"How long have they been renting the Bratton house, Sir John?"

"It is going on two months now, Edward. Has your sister not communicated with you and told you of their situation?"

"No, Sir John, they have not. So they have lost everything. I have not seen nor heard from my sister Fanny since our mother's funeral."

"They seem different, Edward—not so condescending but more humble."

"Well, it seems like their retribution has made them aware of what they have put others through. I am happy for them if it is so, for money is not the most important in life. I learned that the hard way, Sir John."

"Have you seen Robert and Lucy?"

"No, Sir John, they do not keep company with us. It would be nice to see them if they are to be amiable."

"Oh my, Edward, it is hot out here, is it not?"

"Please, Sir John, rest yourself. May I bring you any food or drink?"

"Thank you, my dear fellow. I would like some lemonade."

"Coming right up."

* * * * *

"How have you been, Mrs. Jennings?" asked Elinor.

"Oh, Mrs. Ferrars, not as well as I would like."

"Is there anything I may do or get for you?"

"That is very fine of you, Mrs. Ferrars. I think I would like a tall glass of water."

"Very good. I shall return."

"Thank you, Mrs. Ferrars. I have been sitting here enjoying, watching the young people and remembering the first time I met you and your lovely family."

"We have a good lot of children and young people at our parish."

"Indeed you do, Mrs. Ferrars."

"You know how I am. What can you tell me about Isabella Linton?"

"Well, she was adopted at age 2 by Sir Linton and his late wife. She is an excellent student and has an apprenticeship under her father."

"An apprenticeship for a lady? She must be part of the progressive charter."

"I believe so. We have several young ladies as well as teachers who are part of the same. My nephew Abel has an attachment with her."

"Oh! How wonderful for him—brains and beauty. She is a beautiful young lady, is she not, Mrs. Ferrars?"

"Yes, she is, Mrs. Jennings."

"She has a familiarity about her—the dark hair, dark eyes, and slightly olive skin. She reminds me of someone, but I cannot remember who."

"Perhaps she has dark features like her parents did, Mrs. Jennings."

"Yes, Mrs. Ferrars, you may be right. It seems that Sir Linton has done a wonderful thing when he adopted Isabella."

"I am in agreement with you, Mrs. Jennings. We love Isabella as if she were our own."

"Ahh, here comes your beautiful daughter Kennedi."

"Good afternoon, Mrs. Jennings. So happy to see you and Sir John."

"Thank you, Kennedi. It is lovely to see you also."

"Mama, should I inquire if anyone desires a cup of tea?"

"Yes, dearest, although it may be a bit too warm for tea."

"Mrs. Jennings, would you like a cup of tea?"

"No, thank you, Kennedi. I believe I will continue with my water."

"Very well. I shall continue on my way then."

"Mrs. Ferrars, has Kennedi an attachment with anyone at this time?"

"As a matter of fact, she and William Pendergrast have an understanding."

"Our doctor's name is John Pendergrast. Is William his son?

"Yes, Mrs. Jennings, he is."

"William is currently in practicum between the university and his father. He has two more years before he finishes his residency. By that time, Kennedi will be finished with her studies, and they will plan their wedding."

"Oh, how exciting, Mrs. Ferrars. You and Parson Edward have done a wonderful job with your children. Now what of Brody?"

"Brody is our curious child. He questions everything. Edward and I believe he might be a scientist."

"Oh my, how exciting. Where is your husband, Mrs. Ferrars?"

"I believe he is over by Sir Linton and Colonel Brandon."

"Ahh yes, I see him. I am so glad to see such happiness in your family."

"Thank you, Mrs. Jennings, you are very kind. I would call him to us, but he looks very involved in a conversation."

* * * * *

"Gentlemen," said Edward. "I am happy you both were able to be here for our picnic today."

"Well," said Sir Linton. "Our presence here today is a bit calculated."

"How so?" asked Edward.

"Edward, you and Elinor have been stewards of this land and faithful servants to our parish for these many years."

"Thank you, Colonel. I consider it an honor and blessing to have been chosen as the parson for Delaford."

"Edward Ferrars, your reward has finally arrived."

"My reward, Colonel? What do you mean?"

"This parish, parsonage, and 150 acres now belong to you and Elinor. Sir Linton has finalized the papers, and all that is needed is your and Elinor's signature of acceptance."

"Colonel, what a blessing! I am speechless. Thank you so much for your extraordinary kindness."

"You are very welcome, Edward. You and Elinor truly deserve this."

"Elinor!" shouted Edward.

"Yes, dearest, what is it?"

"Come here quickly."

Mrs. Jennings carefully studied the meeting between Edward and Elinor when she went to him. All of a sudden, they were embracing and shaking hands with the colonel. She wondered what was going on but definitely knew it to be an exciting occasion.

"Colonel," said Edward. "What a blessing you have bestowed upon our family. Thank you so very much."

"On the contrary, you and your family have been an immense blessing to us and the community. Let us celebrate with a toast."

* * * * *

Isabella gave Abel the signal to meet her at the covered bridge.

Abel looks around to make sure that no one is watching him walk off.

"Psst, Abel. Over here."

Abel started laughing.

"Hush! It is not funny!"

"Oh, Miss Isabella, it is very funny. Are you pretending to be a bush?"

"What! No! You need to help me. My dress is caught on the fencing."

"Well, Miss Linton, let us see what can be done."

"Hurry, Abel, before someone sees us."

"Do not trouble yourself, my fair lady, for I am here to rescue you."

As soon as the dress was loosened, Isabella lost her footing and fell onto Abel. They both stood still, looking into each other's eyes as if they were the only two people on earth. A rude fish splashing in the brook brought them back to their circumstance.

"Thank you, Abel."

"You are most welcome, Issy."

"Issy? You must not call me that, Abel."

"And why not?"

"Because it is a term of endearment and not proper in public."

"Ahh, my dear Issy, not a problem, for we are currently not in public."

"Yes, I can see that. Come, let us sit on this bench for our discussion," said Isabella.

"Our discussion?" asked Abel.

"I want to discuss further the Mr. Willoughby situation."

"What is left to discuss, Isabella?"

"Abel, did you not hear all that was discussed with us?"

"Of course, I did. What are you referring to?"

Isabella looked around to make sure that there was not anyone listening. "Abel, do you remember when your father was speaking on Beth?"

"You mean the girl that was with child because of Willoughby?"

"Yes, yes, her."

"What of her? Papa said she died many years ago."

"Yes, I know. My question is what happened to Willoughby's child that she carried?"

"The child?" asked Abel. "Isabella, what does it matter? It is all in the past."

"I understand, but did Beth have the child, and if so, what happened to it?" asked Isabella with a concerned look upon her face.

"I do not know, Isabella. It does not concern us. Papa asked that we not speak about this."

"Oh, you are such a man!" replied Isabella.

All of a sudden, they heard Addison calling out Isabella's name.

"Come, Issy, we must get back to the picnic."

"Abel, you do realize that I cannot let go without knowing what has happened to Beth's baby."

"Shoosh, someone will hear you," said Abel. "Look, Miss Isabella, my mother is waving for us to come to her. Shall we?"

"Very well, but I am not done with this mystery."

"Oh, you are such a stubborn female!" responded Abel. "Mama, did you need me?"

"No, dearest, I saw you and Miss Isabella walking and wondered where you came from."

Isabella quickly answered, "We came from the covered bridge, Mrs. Brandon."

"The covered bridge?" repeated Marianne.

"Yes, Mrs. Brandon. I had some cake scraps and thought it would be fun to feed the fish."

Abel just glared at Isabella, for he did not realize that she could draw out a lie so quickly.

"Miss Linton," asked Miss Dashwood. "What has happened to the hem of your dress?"

"Oh, it got caught on a nail from the bridge, and Mr. Brandon was kind enough to discharge it for me."

As she was talking, Isabella remembered herself falling against Abel, and the special feeling came to her again. She felt her heart pounding and her cheeks feeling warm.

"Miss Isabella," asked Marianne. "Are you well?"

"Yes, Mrs. Brandon, I am well. If you will excuse me, I am going to get a glass of lemonade."

Abel also decided he was thirsty and followed Isabella to get lemonade.

Mrs. Dashwood made an observation about how lovely a pair Isabella and her grandson Abel made. "Is it not so, Marianne?"

"Yes, Mama, I am in agreement. Ever since Isabella was a small child, Abel has had a special attachment for her. I believe he loves her."

"I agree with you, dearest. Isabella is a beautiful young lady. I understand that Sir Linton has made her his apprentice. Have I been informed correctly?" asked Mrs. Dashwood.

"Yes, Mama. Sir Linton is somewhat of a progressive himself and wants his daughter to always have the sensibility and means to take care of herself if need be."

"I truly believe," said Miss Margaret, "that Isabella will establish herself well in life. I also believe that she and Abel have an attachment with each other and may soon have an understanding."

"Margaret," asked Marianne. "Are you aware of an arrangement between them?"

"No, no, dear sister. I am just making an observation. I believe that providence put these two together."

"You may be correct, Margaret," replied Marianne. "I should be very happy to have Isabella as my daughter-in-law, for I truly care for her."

* * * * *

Edward was ringing the bell to signal the beginning of games.

"All right, children, gather around. You must each take a kite and stand apart enough for ease of flying. The one whose kite flies the highest, without having fallen, will be the winner."

"Mrs. Ferrars, did not Brody win the kite-flying event two years in succession?" asked Mrs. Jennings.

"Yes, he did, Mrs. Jennings. He has practiced for weeks in anticipation for this event. He proudly displays his blue ribbons for all his events conquered. Our Brody has much success in all he does."

The picnic was coming to a close. Everyone was seated and singing songs. Kennedi was very happy because William was able to partake. He was seated with the Ferrars family. Sir Linton and Isabella, the Brandons, Mrs. Jennings, and Sir Middleton were sitting together and relishing in a wonderful day.

11

John and Sophia Willoughby

A good foundation in any home must always be built with love. Neither money nor greed nor jealousy nor the first circle can make a relationship bloom. Existing for money is most important for some. What is then left when all has been acquired?

The marriage of John Willoughby to Sophia Grey was in perfect timing for him. His desperate desire for funds carried him into a marriage with no affection. His impertinent behavior led him to irrational behavior. Did his wife know of his former relationships, or did she give into the first man who would have her despite his motivation? Marrying Sophia Grey afforded John Willoughby the opportunity to be included in the first circle.

The Willoughbys, which included John, Sophia, and their only child, Millicent, resided at Combe Magna in Somersetshire. It was a house of great size with the usual number of servants required by each family member.

Millicent, their daughter, had a governess named Mrs. Schremmer. She attended Allenham Academy and seemed to not be a happy child. She was pretentious and rude when necessary. She spent much time alone, for her mama and papa were constantly swirling about in the first circle. Not much love had been shown to her by her parents. If it was not for Mrs. Schremmer, Millicent's governess, she would not have any attention at all. Mrs. Schremmer had been Millicent's governess since she was a baby.

Her mother, Sophia, never really seemed to bond with her own child. She was always too occupied with her social duties. This seemed to be a generational situation due to Sophia's mother and father being detached from her as well.

Her father, John Willoughby, never was affectionate with Sophia, so his nonbonding with his own daughter came easily to him. This conduct seemed to be a pattern with Mr. Willoughby since he left another child as well. His prior conduct had been hidden very well, apparently, for no mention of that was included in any discussion within the Willoughby home.

Millicent had a nervous disposition, for she heard her parents having many disagreements. Millicent was not alone to the awful discussions that go on. Their servants were guarded, for they do not want to be scolded during or after these disagreements. At least Millicent had Mrs. Schremmer to help her when this happened.

"Where are you going, John?" asked Sophia.

"I am riding to see Sir Linton," replied John.

"Sir Linton?" bellowed Sophia.

"Yes, I have business with him."

"What business?" asked Sophia.

"It is not your concern, Sophia," answered Willoughby.

"Not my concern!" yelled Sophia.

As Willoughby walked out, he yelled, "That is true—not your concern!"

Sophia watched as he rode off and wondered why he was to see a barrister.

* * * * *

As John Willoughby arrived at Sir Linton's, he saw Isabella outside with her horse, Thunder.

"Good morning, Miss Linton," said Willoughby.

Isabella whipped around, startled. "Mr. Willoughby. Can I help you?"

"I am sorry to have frightened you," responded Willoughby. "Yes, you may help me. I need to speak to Sir Linton."

No sooner did Willoughby finish his request than Sir Linton quickly opened the door and came to Willoughby. "May I help you?" asked Sir Linton.

"It was very nice to see you again, Miss Linton," said Willoughby.

Isabella said nothing but did display half a smile.

"Come, Mr. Willoughby, we shall go to my office."

Isabella felt troubled while being around Willoughby. *Why should he be here? What does he desire?* thought Isabella.

"Mr. Willoughby, what can I do for you?" asked Sir Linton.

"I would like to transfer my business to your office, if possible," replied Willoughby.

"Mr. Willoughby, I am not certain that I may take on any more clients. I will look upon my schedule and give you my decision within a fortnight," answered Sir Linton.

"Very well, Sir Linton. I look forward to your reply," said Willoughby.

Sir Linton casually looked outside to make sure Isabella was not there. "Yes, thank you," said Sir Linton.

As soon as Willoughby left, Sir Linton went out to look for Isabella.

"Miss Wall, have you seen Isabella?" asked Sir Linton.

"Yes, sir. She has already departed for the academy," replied Miss Wall.

"Thank you, Miss Wall."

When Willoughby returned home, he saw an unusual carriage in front of his house. *Who could this be?* Willoughby thought to himself.

As he walked into the house, he recognized the voice to be that of his cousin Ashby Wilton. *Why is Ashby speaking to Sophia?* he wondered.

"Well, well, greetings, cousin," said Ashby with a smirk upon his smug face.

"What are you doing here, Ashby?" asked Willoughby.

"I have come to meet your lovely wife," said Ashby.

"John, why have you never mentioned your cousin Ashby before?" asked Sophia.

"Because after he took all of Lady Allen's inheritance, he left her alone and disappeared," replied Willoughby.

"Now, now, Mr. Willoughby, if anyone does well at disappearing, it would be you," said Ashby.

Willoughby's eyes widened with every word Ashby spoke.

"What does he refer to, John?" asked Sophia.

"It is not of any value," replied Willoughby. "Why are you really here, Ashby?" asked Willoughby again.

"To meet my cousin's family, of course. Is this all your family, John?" asked Ashby.

"No, Millicent is at her studies upstairs," replied Willoughby.

"Ahh, your daughter with Sophia," spewed Ashby.

"So, Ashby, where have you been keeping yourself all these years?" asked Willoughby.

Sophia sat very still and with unease on the davenport, listening to this question-and-answer moment. She felt as if something was not quite right. *What are these two men not saying?* thought Sophia.

"Well, I have been living a bit here and there. I lived the longest in Kennsington," replied Ashby. "I met a mutual acquaintance of ours there, Willoughby. Perhaps you might remember Ms. Beth Williams."

"What is going on, John?" asked Sophia.

"Do not concern yourself with this dribble, Sophia," replied Willoughby.

"My dear cousin, have you not apprised your wife of Beth?" said Ashby.

"Ashby, I believe it is time for you to leave to wherever you came from!" said Willoughby with anger in his voice.

Sophia asked John, "Who is Beth?"

"Very well, Willoughby, I will leave. Oh, let me offer my congratulations on you having another daughter," said Ashby.

Both Sophia and Willoughby whipped their heads around in surprise to this revelation.

"What! What are you referring to, Ashby?" demanded Willoughby.

"I had a long conversation with our sweet Beth, and she revealed to me how you left her with child, never to be seen again. You have a wonderful baby girl from what I saw of her when she was two years of age," replied Ashby.

"Get out now, you rogue!" demanded Willoughby.

Meanwhile, Sophia fell onto the davenport with her face in her hands. At the same time this discussion was happening, Millicent was concealed behind the library pocket doors, listening to all that had transpired. She sat on the floor with her knees to her chest and her arms wrapped around them, rocking back and forth.

"Very well, Willoughby, I am leaving now. Oh, by the way, Beth died when the baby girl was two years of age. She was adopted in Sussex—in case you are interested," said Ashby.

"I have no interest in what you say, Ashby," said Willoughby.

"You should also know that I lost trace of her. Seems that her adoption documentation has been secured very well. Sounds as if someone wanted to ensure she would not be found. This, Mrs. Willoughby, is the motivation for Lady Allen's tossing out Willoughby without his inheritance. I see, from looking about, that Willoughby has secured his wealth from you. Lucky chap, I say. Well, my task is done, and I must be on my way. Good luck, ole chap." Ashby smiled.

As Ashby was speaking, Willoughby and Sophia stood in silence with fright and panic all about Willoughby's face.

Soft whimpering could be heard from between the crack of the pocket doors to the library. The cries were lost upon her parents, for nothing else occupied their silence. When Ashby departed, he had a self-congratulatory gaze upon him.

As the door slammed with Ashby's departure, Sophia demanded that Willoughby inform her of all the particulars concerning Beth Williams. Willoughby had no intention of revealing any particulars to her or anyone else.

"I will not stand here and respond to your demands. My past is none of your concern. We, my dear, are finished for this evening!" shouted Willoughby.

"Yes, Mr. Willoughby, we are finished, and not just for this evening," replied Sophia.

"What are you referring to now, Sophia?" asked Willoughby.

"If you don't explain to me of your indiscretion, then I shall have Barrister Henley stop all my funding for you," replied Sophia.

"You, my dear, cannot hold me accountable for my prior actions, for it was before I had an attachment with you," responded Willoughby.

"I am still waiting for your clarification, John," replied Sophia.

Willoughby thought very carefully about his decision to disclose his explanation. "Very well!" bellowed Willoughby. I was involved with a young lady by the name of Beth Williams. After staying with her for a time, she told me that she was with child. I could not stay, for I was young and not ready for children. I left without telling her and went to stay with my aunt, Lady Allen. I was told by my aunt that I was to inherit when she passed. At the same time, I met another young lady called Marianne Dashwood. Lady Allen found me out about Beth and sent me off from Allenham," said Willoughby.

"So you have left two women in despair. This must have been when you searched me out. My money is what you desired, not me," said Sophia.

"You did not suffer being with me, dearest," replied Willoughby.

"This whole charade of a marriage was all about my funding your desires," said Sophia.

Meanwhile, Millicent opened the pocket door, crying and screaming that she hates her parents as she ran upstairs. Both Sophia and Willoughby just stood there in amazement, for they knew not that she was listening to everything that was said.

"What are we to do with our daughter Sophia?" asked Willoughby.

"You had best concern yourself with what I might do with you, sir," replied Sophia.

"Sophia, do you not care about our daughter?" asked Willoughby.

"Mrs. Schremmer will handle her—that is her job," answered Sophia. "Where is this other daughter that your cousin spoke of?"

"I do not know. I have not seen Beth for many years," answered Willoughby.

Meanwhile, upstairs, Mrs. Schremmer was comforting Millie. Everyone in the household heard the disruptive discussion.

"Mr. Willoughby, I will be visiting Barrister Henley day after tomorrow, so you need to prepare yourself, sir!" bellowed Sophia.

Willoughby stood in silence with his thoughts and needed to think of a plan to help himself.

12

The Birthday Gala

Today was the first day of March—and what an exciting time it was—for it was the start of the organization of Isabella's eighteenth birthday gala. Isabella needed this diversion from all that had been going on especially with John Willoughby. Addison and Kennedi were to come to Linton Park to help her with her birthday gala.

Isabella heard someone knocking on the front door and ran all the way down the stairs.

"Wait, Miss Wall," asked Isabella. "I am expecting my friends. Please let me answer the door."

"Miss Isabella, I am glad to see that you have dressed for this occasion of answering the door," said Miss Wall.

"You are so amusing, Miss Wall," said Isabella.

Isabella finally reached the front door. She straightened her dress and then went to open the door. As she opened the door, she yelled out, "Welcome to my gala arrangement!"

On the outside, there stood John Willoughby. "Miss Linton, you seem very excited today. Is Sir Linton in his office?" asked Willoughby.

Isabella stood there without moving or saying a word.

Sir Linton quickly came from behind Isabella and requested she go upstairs to wait for her acquaintances.

"Mr. Willoughby, what can I do for you?" asked Sir Linton.

"Sir Linton, I am in desperate need of counsel!" stated Willoughby.

"Come in, and follow me to my office. Please have a seat."

Isabella ran up the stairs as quickly as possible, her heart beating fast and palms sweating. She wondered why this man got her so unsettled. As she looked out her bedroom window, she saw the barouche which carried Addison and Kennedi. This time she would allow Benson or Miss Wall to answer the door, for she did not want to engage with Willoughby again.

"So, Mr. Willoughby, what has happened?" asked Sir Linton.

"My wife, Sophia, and I have had a terrible quarrel. She has threatened me with the removal of my funds, and I would like to see what can be done about it."

"What is the name of your wife's barrister?" asked Sir Linton.

"She mentioned a Barrister Henley of Chelsea," answered Willoughby.

"Ahh, yes, Roger Henley. I thought he had been removed from our profession a few years back, but apparently not," replied Sir Linton.

"Well, Sir Linton, can you take me on?" asked Willoughby.

"Mr. Willoughby, consider this interview gratis. My stipend for this situation can be between 250 to 1,000 pounds, depending on the amount of investigation necessary to put an end to your predicament," replied Sir Linton.

"Yes, yes, of course," said Mr. Willoughby.

"I suggest you immediately visit your bank and place a draft in the amount of five hundred pounds as soon as you depart my office, for Mrs. Willoughby will not wait to set you up," suggested Sir Linton.

"Of course, Sir Linton. Should I return here with the funds?" asked Willoughby.

"No, sir. I must go to town and start your paperwork, so meet me at the courthouse around three o'clock," replied Sir Linton.

"Thank you, Sir Linton, for your expedited service. Please tell Miss Linton goodbye for me and that it was good to see her," said Willoughby.

"Very well, Mr. Willoughby, I will see you shortly. Goodbye," said Sir Linton.

The whole time he was talking with Willoughby, he was pondering on how much of a cad this man was. *And no, I shall not pass on your message to my daughter.*

* * * * *

"Ahh, Kennedi, Addison, how lovely it is to see you ladies," said Sir Linton.

"Thank you, Sir Linton," replied both ladies.

"Papa, we are so excited, for Miss Wall has brought us several small cakes to choose from for my gala."

"That is wonderful, dearest. I must leave to go to the courthouse. Please continue with your objective, and do have fun, ladies."

"Thank you, Papa."

"All right, ladies, into the kitchen we go for our tasting!" said Miss Wall.

"Oh my goodness, this lemon pound cake is heavenly," remarked Kennedi.

"Why, yes, it is, Kennedi. It also would suit as a wedding cake," said Addison.

All the ladies began to giggle.

"It is settled, Miss Wall. We shall have the lemon pound cake with lavender buttercream icing," said Isabella.

"What of the meat, Isabella?" asked Miss Wall.

"Well, we have given it a lot of thought and have decided on roast of beef, lamb chops, and ham," replied Isabella.

"Oh my, that sounds wonderful. Let us also have crackers from cheese, grapes, and strawberries," suggested Addison.

"Do not forget the chocolate," said Kennedi.

"All these foods sound wonderful. I would also like lavender ice cream, Miss Wall," said Isabella.

"What of the flowers?" asked Miss Wall.

"We have decided on purple and pink irises with decorative grasses and pink roses on the table for the presents," replied Isabella.

"I believe that to be great choices for the flowers. Don't forget your bouquet, which will be pink roses, Miss Isabella," replied Miss Wall.

"Now what of the invitation list?" asked Miss Wall.

"I have made my list, and Papa has made his. I need to discuss a certain guest with my friends, then it will be done," replied Isabella.

"Very well, Miss Isabella. We will get together after lunch for the final plan," said Miss Wall.

"Ladies, let us go out to the garden for our discussion," suggested Isabella.

"I do not know how to approach this guest with you two ladies," said Isabella.

"Who is it?" asked Kennedi.

"I have been pondering on asking Millicent to my gala."

"What—why?" bellowed Addison.

"I don't know what it is about her, but I feel a peculiar bond for her. I believe she desperately needs attention and is not receiving any at all," explained Isabella.

"You have a kind heart, Isabella," said Kennedi.

"Very well, we shall all be in agreement and follow your heart as well," spoke Addison.

"Addison, are you aware that Andrew will be coming?" said Isabella.

"I am, and I am glad of it, ladies," replied Addison.

"Kennedi, William has accepted my invitation, so all will be well," said Isabella.

"How wonderful! I have not seen William for a month. He has been working at Mercy Hospital."

"Anyone else to ask about Miss Isabella?" teased Kennedi.

"No, I believe two hundred guests shall suffice," said Isabella.

"Two hundred guests! Have you invited every person in the county?" laughed Addison.

"Papa had his own list of close acquaintances but only after my recommendations."

"So there will be several ladies and lords, I assume?" asked Kennedi.

"Of course. Papa is of the finest and travels easily within the first circle," replied Isabella.

"Well, now, we have confirmed the food, the flowers, the music, and guests. What is left?" asked Addison.

"Nothing. Now we wait for May 1st," replied Kennedi.

* * * * *

Isabella had dispatched an invitation to Millicent Willoughby but has had no response as of yet. Isabella truly did want Millie to come, for she believed that she may have a wonderful evening.

The day had finally arrived. It was the day of Isabella's birthday gala. As she lay on her bed, she admired her beautiful gown that her papa had commissioned for her. It would soon be time to put on the gown and walk downstairs to the ballroom with her papa by her side.

"Miss Isabella, Addison and Kennedi have arrived. They are on their way up," announced Miss Wall.

"Thank you," said Isabella. The door flew open, and in came Kennedi and Addison.

"Where are Miss Ginger and Miss Crenshaw, ladies?" asked Isabella.

"They are downstairs with Miss Wall. She needed extra help, and they were kind enough to volunteer," said Addison.

"Isabella, have you been given a response to your gala from Millie?" asked Addison.

"No, I have not heard a word. I do hope she will come."

"Well, my dear friends, we need to get dressed. It will soon be time to go downstairs," said Isabella.

"I hope we do not fall when we go down the stairs," said Kennedi.

"Are you anxious, Isabella?" asked Addison.

"I might be a bit," admitted Isabella.

"I wonder if our boys are downstairs yet," said Kennedi.

"Could be," replied Isabella.

"Isabella, your guests have arrived. You, Kennedi, and Addison have ten minutes until you need to appear," called Miss Wall.

"My, Isabella, what a beautiful dress, and it looks so lovely on you," replied Kennedi.

"Thank you, dear friend. You both look very lovely also."

"I hear the music, ladies. It is now time to gather and go downstairs," said Addison.

Down the stairs came Addison, Kennedi, then finally the birthday girl on her papa's arm. They walked slowly into the ballroom with their bouquets in their hands.

Abel's eyes became large when he laid eyes on Isabella. His heart was pounding and could think of nothing else but how much he wanted to dance with her. Isabella looked upon him with her smile, and his heart seemed to melt. William and Andrew also gave admiring glances to Kennedi and Addison as their eyes looked upon each other.

After being announced, Isabella began her search for Millie. *Where could she be?* she thought to herself.

Everyone began clapping, and all the guests wished her a happy birthday at once. Isabella curtsied and thanked everyone. Abel immediately made his way up to see Isabella.

"My dear Isabella, how beautiful you are."

"Why, thank you, Mr. Brandon. I am so pleased that you are here. We shall have many dances together."

"Well, dearest, I shall let you now attend to your gala. I must make my way to my acquaintances," said Sir Linton.

"Thank you so much, Papa, for everything. I just adore it all."

Sir Linton took Isabella's hand and lightly kissed it. "You are most welcome, dearest."

"Abel, there are so many people here," remarked Isabella.

"Yes, dearest. All these people care for you and want to celebrate your birthday with you."

"Have you seen Millie, Abel?"

"Millie! Why should she be here when she does not care for you."

"She is not a happy girl, and I have sorrow for her. Oh, wait, there she is! Who are those ladies with her?" asked Isabella. "Miss Wall, come here please."

"Miss Isabella, what can I do for you?"

"Do you see Millicent Willoughby over there?

"Yes, dear, why?" responded Miss Wall.

"Who are those two ladies with her?"

"Oh, that is Mrs. Schremmer, Millie's governess, and her mother, Mrs. Willoughby."

"Thank you, Miss Wall."

"Abel, I must go and welcome Millie. Excuse me."

* * * * *

"Millie, how wonderful it is to see you. Thank you for coming," said Isabella.

"Thank you for inviting me, Isabella. This is my mother, Sophia Willoughby, and Mrs. Schremmer, my governess."

"Mrs. Willoughby, Mrs. Schremmer. It is a pleasure to meet you both. Thank you for bringing Millie."

"Happy birthday, Miss Isabella. I have never seen such a grand birthday gala with so many guests. We are happy to be here to celebrate your birthday. What is your age?" asked Sophia.

"I am eighteen today."

Millie was standing with her head down. Isabella found it in her heart to inquire quietly about Millie.

"Millie, come with me. I want to show you my cake."

As the girls walked toward the cake, Isabella asked Millie about what was troubling her.

"Isabella, will you take a turn with me?"

"Of course, dear. Let us go and sit in Papa's office. We will not be disturbed there."

* * * * *

"What is it, Millie? Can I help you?" asked Isabella.

"I want to say to you, Isabella, that I am so sorry for how I have treated you. You are everything I want to be and have much love in your life. I believe that I was jealous."

"Millie, I feel it in my heart that you are unhappy. Is this true?"

"Yes, Isabella, I am very unhappy. My mother and father have confrontations all the time. I feel that they do not love each other or me. I found out last week that I have a half sister somewhere because my father abandoned a lady with his child many years ago. My mother has never been loving to me. She is always out gaining status in the first circle along with my father. We have not ever gone anywhere as a family."

"Oh my goodness, Millie. I am so sorry to hear of that. Please know that I desire to be a close friend and want to help you in any situation you desire."

Isabella's heart was breaking for Millie, but she did not show it, for she wanted to be strong for her.

Millie began to weep. Isabella took her into her arms and comforted her till she was calm.

"Let us go back to my gala arm in arm as good friends do. Let us show you off, for you are very pretty this evening, Millie."

"I would like that very much, Isabella."

"Then it is done. We shall eat, dance, and laugh, for it is a good thing to do. We shall find Kennedi and Addison so we may be among friends," said Isabella.

"Oh, are you in earnest, Isabella?"

"Most sincerely," she said.

Millie and Isabella embraced and smiled at each other then went to the ballroom to join the others. Everyone was enjoying themselves, and Isabella wanted to ensure that Millie would have the best time ever.

Isabella led Millie to her group known as "circle of friends."

"Ladies and gentlemen, here is my new friend, Millie. She is here to share my birthday with me. Millie is now part of our 'circle of friends.' "Does anyone have an objection?"

Everyone standing in the circle did not dare to object, for they know of Isabella's heart and her good judgment. In the circle stood Abel, Addison, Kennedi, William, and Andrew.

"Welcome, Millie," said all. "We are happy to have you in our circle."

"If we can ever help you, please let us know," said Kennedi.

"Thank you all for your kindness," said Millie.

Abel leaned against Isabella and Millie to say something wonderful is about to happen.

At that very moment, William walked over to Kennedi, took her hands into his as he kneeled. He then told her that he loved her very much and wanted to share his life with her.

"Will you marry me, Kennedi Ferrars?"

Kennedi's eyes began to tear up. "Yes, dearest, I most definitely will marry you, for I love you also."

Everyone started to cheer and embrace the newly engaged couple. Edward, Elinor, and Brody offered their congratulations and love. Isabella smiled at Abel with her eyes, thanking him for welcoming Millie into their circle.

It was time for the young ladies and gentlemen who are friends of Isabella to escort her to her presents. As Isabella was sitting, she asked Millie to help her with the presents. This made Millie very happy. Isabella looked upon Millie and saw how happy she was, which brought a tear to her own eye.

Everyone was having such a wonderful time. The evening was magical but drawing to an end. Before Millie left, she ran to Mrs. Schremmer to let her know that she had a wonderful evening. Millie then embraced Mrs. Schremmer even though her mother was standing beside Mrs. Schremmer.

Isabella was watching what was happening with Millie, for she can see who truly cared for Millie.

Millie's mother, Sophia, was going about the ballroom during the party, attempting to speak with anyone who should listen to her but was not getting along with anyone, for they all knew of her and that she desired to be in the first circle. Sir Linton's acquaintances were more humble than the other class of first circles.

* * * * *

"So, dearest, how did you enjoy your gala?" asked her papa.

"It was very lovely, Papa. Thank you so much for all you have done for me."

"You are most welcome, Isabella."

"I see that you have made a new acquaintance of Millicent Willoughby," remarked Sir Linton.

"Yes, Papa. I thought that I should be her friend, for she seemed to be such an unhappy girl. I cannot explain it better than that, Papa."

"So did you enjoy all the gifts you received?" asked Sir Linton.

"Oh yes, Papa."

"Ahh, Abel, still here?" asked Sir Linton.

"Yes, Sir Linton, I stayed behind so that I may give Isabella her gift in private."

"Well, let me get on with what I was doing."

"Oh no, Sir Linton, stay if you desire. I just referred to the many people before."

"What is it, Abel?" asked Isabella.

"What is what…oh, the gift. Pardon me. Here it is. I located it in a shop and thought of you instantly."

"Oh, Abel, how beautiful! I adore it. Look, Papa, is it not beautiful?"

"Yes, dearest, it is a lovely cameo. Bravo, Abel, you have an eye for such things."

"Thank you so much, Abel. I shall treasure it always."

"Well, if you will excuse me, Sir Linton, Miss Isabella, I must be on my way home. Thank you for a wonderful gala, and happy birthday again."

"Goodbye, Abel. I shall hope to see you soon," replied Isabella.

Abel bowed and went on his way.

"Papa, so many gifts. I have not opened them all. I am going to bed, for I am so tired." She stood on her tiptoes and gave her papa a kiss on the cheek.

Isabella carried her gifts from Abel and from Millie to her room. She sat on her bed, looking at the cameo and then brought it to her lips and gave it a kiss. She then opened her gift from Millie. *What a beautiful trinket box*, she thought: The box was made from mahogany wood trimmed with pearls and lavender flowers. When she opened the box, she saw a note inside.

"What is this?"

The note said,

> Thank you for inviting me to your birthday gala. It means a lot to me. I want us to be like sisters in closeness.

Isabella started to weep. She spoke out loud, "We will be like sisters, my dear Millie."

Isabella was overjoyed with the notion of being close to Millie, for she had had so much unhappiness and heartache in her short life. As she lay on her bed, she fell fast asleep clutching the cameo brooch to her chest in one hand and holding the trinket box in the other.

13

The Family Atonement

It had been a week now since the birthday gala. All was well at Edward and Elinor's home. Kennedi was still elated from her proposal from William Pendergrast. Edward had put off having a discussion with Elinor concerning the new circumstances of his sister Fanny and brother Robert. He did not want to sour the elation of his daughter's engagement. Edward had finally decided that after supper tonight would be best to reveal to Elinor the letter from Fanny. Elinor was searching for Brody, so she decided to ask Edward of Brody's whereabouts.

"Have you seen Brody, Edward?"

"Yes, dearest. He is at the lake, catching our supper for this evening," answered Edward.

"Thank you, dear. I shall go and fetch him, for if we are to eat tonight, he must come now."

* * * * *

"Supper was wonderful, thanks be to God, our son, and my dear wife," remarked Edward.

All the dishes were taken up and washed, and the children had gone to bed.

Now would be the perfect time to approach Elinor about the letter, thought Edward.

"Sit with me, my dear, for I have news from Sir Middleton regarding John and Fanny, which is to be quite shocking."

"What do you mean, dearest?"

"Well, Sir John has told me during our church picnic that John and Fanny are leasing a three-bedroom house in Brookshire by name of Bratton House from him and that they have been there for five months now."

"I don't understand. Is it not enough that they have houses in London and Sussex?"

"Not so, dearest. They no longer have the house in London or Sussex. It appears that they have exhausted John's inheritance and can no longer afford the extravagant situation, for it was used up while keeping company in the first circle."

"They must be devastated, Edward, for their whole lives existed solely on attaining the rewards that come from the first circle. I cannot imagine that Fanny is of sound mind with this complete turnabout. All those moments that they exalted themselves above everyone who was beneath them as well as the hurtful things said and did especially when my father passed. It seems that they are now at the same social status as the rest of us. This situation has retribution written all over them. Do you know, my dear, what their notion is in regard to our family?"

"I am not certain, but we may find out soon, for Fanny has written to me and requests an interview with your mama, Marianne, and Margaret."

"I am curious as to what this interview with us all will be about. Has Fanny given a specific day for this visit?"

"She suggested Sunday next, after church service."

"Then Edward, we will accommodate them, for it is the right thing to do. If I may make a suggestion, ask them to come earlier for church service that morning, then we shall have dinner and afterward have the discussion that they requested."

"I believe that to be an excellent suggestion, my dear. Brookshire is not but sixteen miles from here, and we can make a day of it. I will reply to Fanny and John and have Brody take the letter to town tomorrow. They will receive it in plenty of time."

"Very well, dear. I will make sure that mama, Marianne, and Margaret are aware of this situation so that they prepare themselves for their visit on Sunday next. We must also make certain that the children will not disturb us until the visit is suitable for them. I will go and speak to Marianne, Mama, and Margaret tomorrow to make certain that they will be available for our discussion with Fanny and John."

"Thank you, my dear. Let us now retire, for I am exhausted. Tomorrow I will compose my response to Fanny carefully and then continue writing my sermon for Sunday next."

"Edward, I am going to Marianne's so that we may travel together to Barton cottage to speak to Mama and Margaret."

"Very well, dear. The children are home from the academy, and I have sent Brody to town with the letter to Fanny and John. I am also going to Exeter for livestock supplies."

Elinor took the barouche to get Marianne and ride to Barton cottage to speak to her mama and sister Margaret.

* * * * *

"Hello, dear sister, and how are you today?" asked Marianne.

"I am well. Where are Abel and Addison?" replied Elinor.

"They are working on their studies. Are you going to inform me about our visit to Mama?"

"I prefer we wait until we get to Mama's, for I must tell you all together."

"Very well. I should be surprised then. Is Kennedi still elated over her engagement to William?"

"Most definitely. She is already making plans for their wedding day."

"Have they spoken of when they plan on marrying?"

"Well, William still has one year left on his practicum through his father. He has been putting away his money for their marriage. Edward and I were so excited when he asked for Edward's permission to marry Kennedi. We could not have asked for a better man for our

Kennedi. Speaking of proposals, when do you believe that Abel will propose to Isabella?" asked Elinor.

"I do not know, but one thing is for sure—that boy is deeply in love with her and, I believe, she with him. He still has two more years of practicum with Sir Linton through the university. He is very fortunate to have such a wonderful example of the law with Sir Linton."

"I believe it to be providence for those two to be together. They just fulfill each other," said Elinor.

"Yes, I am in agreement. Are you aware that Isabella is under her father's tutelage?"

"What! No. I am not aware of that! She truly is a progressive. She is also a clever and beautiful young lady."

* * * * *

"Hello, Margaret!" yelled Marianne.

"Thank goodness we have finally arrived. Reading another book, Margaret?" asked Elinor.

"Of course, you know me."

"Where is Mama?" asked Marianne.

"She is in the house sewing."

"Where is Melanie, Margaret?" asked Elinor.

"She has gone to Exeter for supplies."

"Very good. Let us go inside, for we have need of a discussion," said Elinor.

"Hello, Mama."

"My darlings, how good to see you both. I have all my girls at home again."

"Mama, let us all go to the table, for we need to have a discussion of some importance."

"Is everything well with your families?"

"Yes, all is fine."

"Margaret, would you please bring us some refreshment?" asked Marianne.

"Of course, dear sister."

"All right, Elinor, you have all of our attention. Out with whatever it is that is of importance," demanded Marianne.

"Very well. At our church picnic, Edward was told by Sir John that John and Fanny were renting Bratton House in Brookshire from him."

Margaret, Marianne, and mama were all looking at each other, for they thought that John and Fanny have obtained a third house, just as Elinor first thought.

"They do not have enough with two homes. Now they have a third. Is there no end to their funds?" asked Mama.

"Wait, Mama, let me finish. Sir John, of course, had to investigate their funding for the rent from John Dashwood, as per law. What he found out was astonishing."

"What are you saying, Elinor?" asked Mama.

"It appears that John and Fanny have gone through his inheritance and, therefore, losing their London home and Norland. They have lost all due to their extravagant life. Sir Linton is John's barrister. Therefore, he was mandated to tell Sir John, the landlord, that there were funds for the amount of money that Sir John was asking for. It appears that John and Fanny have been put on a monthly account through Sir Linton. The law has recovered all that was owed, and therefore, the inheritance, except for your money, Mama, that you receive, has been paid to their creditors. Bratton house is a small house because that is all they are allowed for rent," explained Elinor.

"Well, this reminds me of when Fanny made her comment about our living arrangement when we were forced from Norland and into this cottage. I feel that retribution has made a visit to Mr. and Mrs. Dashwood," exclaimed Mama.

"I cannot believe it! Their actions for all these years has caught up with them," remarked Marianne.

"Margaret, do you not have anything to say?" asked Elinor.

"Not yet, dear sister. I feel you have more to say."

"So, they have been living in Brookshire and have not sent word nor visited us. They must feel shame and embarrassment of their new situation," remarked Mama.

"I have more to tell."

"Ahh, you see. I was right," said Margaret.

"Edward received a letter from Fanny asking for a visit on Sunday next. She also asked if we all can be present at our house for their visit."

"There must be something of great value they want if they requested a particular visit and them in the situation that they are in," said Mama.

"Do you believe that their current situation has humbled them?" asked Marianne.

"I would hope so. We all are the only family they have. I believe that when they were found out, their first circle acquaintances were nowhere to be found. We must show them grace and be the example for them," replied Elinor.

"Oh, one more thing. We invited them to join us for church service then dinner. Afterward, we will engage in our family discussion."

"Everyone needs to be in agreement. We all need to listen to what they have to say, then we may reply accordingly," said Margaret.

"That is a very good suggestion, Margaret. Well, we must be off, for suppertime approaches. Till Sunday, all. Goodbye," said Elinor.

As they were on their way home, they noticed Brody up ahead on his horse. Brody recognized his mama and aunt, so he stopped and waited on them.

"Well, my son, did you get the letter dispatched?"

"Yes, Mama. Greetings, Aunt Marianne."

"Hello, my dear Brody. Are you well today?"

"Yes, Aunt Marianne. Thank you."

"Mama, I have been given another letter for you and Papa."

"Let me see it son. Well, it is from Robert and Lucy out of Hendler Cottage in Werksbury. What could they possibly want, for we have not heard from them in such a long time."

"Hurry, Elinor, and open the letter, for it is addressed to you as well!" said Marianne.

"Oh my!"

"What is it?" asked Marianne.

"Well, it appears that Robert and Lucy have requested a visit with our family as well."

"What!" said Marianne.

"We must hurry home and ask Edward to send another dispatchment for Robert and Lucy."

"What do you think they may want, Elinor?" asked Marianne.

"I do not know, but come Sunday next, we shall be enlightened, I presume."

When Elinor returned home, she quickly looked for Edward, for he needed to reply to his brother's letter.

"Ahh, I thought I might find you with your chickens. Dearest, we have received a letter from Robert and Lucy. They wrote that they desire to visit us."

"Really! It is not usual to have both my sister and brother send me letters this close together. I feel that their wanting to visit is of importance—spiritually, that is."

"My darling, you have always been blessed with spiritual notions. That is why your sermons are from your heart and our parishioners are the better for it."

"You are very kind, my love. You must hurry, dearest, for you need to respond to Robert today. I will alert Brody that he will need to return to town with your letter."

"Very well. I am finished here. Let me go now and quickly respond. I will write that we would like for them to visit at the same time as John and Fanny with the same circumstances."

As Sunday was approaching, Elinor and Kennedi were preparing the two empty bedrooms with fresh linens in case their soon-to-come family decided to stay the night. Edward was deep in thought concerning his sermon for tomorrow, for he wanted his words to relate to family and the love within.

* * * * *

Morning had arrived, and the anticipation of Edward's family was causing a bit of nervousness. It was a beautiful sunny day with the lovely aroma of flowers from the beautiful garden surrounding the Ferrars home. All the rooms now had flowers placed in them along with the crisp linens that were given to Elinor from her mother-in-law, Mrs. Ferrars. The dinner had been prepared for after the service. All of a sudden, Brody came running into the house to let his papa know that there were two carriages coming up their road.

"Elinor, I believe our family is arriving at the same moment, for there are two carriages."

"Yes, dearest, I can see them from the kitchen window."

"Kennedi, Brody, hurry and come down, for your aunts and uncles have arrived. Please present yourselves outside and welcome them in, for we have a bit of time before church begins."

"Yes, Mama, we are on our way!"

The children were outside, welcoming their aunts and uncles, as Edward and Elinor were preparing themselves inside.

"Good morning, one and all. Happy to have you all in our home," said Edward.

Good morning was said by all.

"Please come in and sit down. We are preparing ourselves for church service. We are happy that you good folk will join us. After service, we will have dinner, then we can all have our discussion that you all requested…if this is agreeable?" asked Edward.

"That is a wonderful proposal," replied Fanny.

"Edward, your home is very large and lovely," remarked Lucy.

"Thank you, Lucy. We have, over the years, built on two more bed chambers and a larger kitchen for our growing family. As a welcoming, Elinor and Kennedi have prepared for you the two empty bed chambers should you desire to stay the night with us."

"Why, thank you Elinor. That is very kind of you," said Fanny.

"You are most welcome, Fanny. May I get anyone tea before we go to church service?" asked Elinor.

As Elinor was preparing the tea in the kitchen, Fanny came in to help.

"Elinor, do you not have a cook?"

"Most definitely, Fanny, but we offer Sundays off to our servants so they may spend time with their families."

"That is a very kind gesture, Elinor. I am certain that it pleases them."

"Yes, it does, Fanny. Thank you."

"Here, Elinor, let me help you with the tea."

"Thank you, Fanny."

Elinor noticed a change in Fanny like never before. She has never offered to help in anything before. *Is this a new plan, or has Fanny actually become a better person?* wondered Elinor.

Meanwhile, Edward was enjoying pleasantries with his brother Robert, Lucy, and John.

"Well, my dear family, now that we have finished our tea, let us proceed to church service. I have reserved a pew up front alongside my family for you all."

"That is very kind of you," said Robert.

In the church, pleasantries were given by all the family including Marianne, her family, Mrs. Dashwood, and Margaret.

Edward spoke on the bond and love of family through God's Word. Everyone was appreciative of Edward's sermon today. The sermon came straight from Edward's heart, for everyone knew him to be an honest and kind man.

Church service was over, and it was time for Sunday dinner and then time for the discussion that Fanny and Robert desired.

"That was a wonderful supper, my dear."

"Thank you, dearest. I know how much you like roast of beef," said Elinor.

Fanny, John, Robert, and Lucy were all listening and observing Edward's family. They all seemed genuinely fascinated on how Edward's family are so happy and loving with each other. By the looks on their faces, it seems that Fanny and the rest want the same for their respective family. It was now time for the family discussion to begin. Edward made sure that they would not be disturbed by Kennedi or Brody. He asked for everyone involved to see their way to the parlor and to be seated. Edward than seated himself by Elinor while offering to begin the discussion.

"Dear family, we are so glad to have you here all together. It has been past due time for this family to share and love as one. I have said my piece, so if anyone would like to start speaking, please do so."

Everyone sat silent for a moment while they glanced at each other with smiles, which is a hopeful indication on how the discussion will progress.

Fanny stood up and spoke with a slight trembling voice.

"Dear family, we have come today to endear ourselves to you all. We have been made to realize that John and I both have been unkind and not fair to our family. We have lost everything we had due to our excessive squander on things that—we know now—did not matter. All that mattered, we thought, was to be in the first circle. Well, our first circle let us go due to our current situation. Mrs. Dashwood, Elinor, Marianne, and Margaret, your father wanted to leave you girls something for your dowry, but I talked John into not giving any to you at all. I am with great shame and pray that you all will forgive us for the many wrong doings that we have done to you, our family. We desire greatly to be part of this family, for all we have is each other. I read my mother's letter many times before I finally understood what it was she was trying to tell me. Please, if you can find it in your hearts to forgive us, we shall live the rest of our lives making a better situation for us all."

John went over to Fanny, for she started to cry. Mrs. Dashwood, Elinor, Marianne, and Margaret all took a turn to comfort, therefore forgiving Fanny and John.

Edward said, "We are all very blessed and will now have my sister and her husband back with us. Thank you both for your truth. We all will forgive you both."

"Thank you all for your extraordinary kindness to us. We shall truly be a family now," said Fanny.

Robert and Lucy looked upon each other, for they both knew what they needed to do. They both stood up and walked to the center of the parlor.

"We also have lost everything. Our greed took us over and had blinded us from what is truly important. Edward, Mama should have never taken away your inheritance, for it was wrong of her. She had written me a letter also explaining what is the right manner of things to do. It was not until we lost all that we realized what is truly important. We are truly sorrowful for anything that we have done against you and ask your forgiveness. We, like Fanny and John, want Lucy and myself to live in peace and love."

Edward stood again and went to shake Robert's hand and embraced Lucy. The rest of the family followed with cheerful embraces. Elinor invited Fanny, John, Robert, and Lucy to stay the night so they may catch up on the joys of the family news.

"We have joyous news. Our Kennedi is engaged to William Pendergrast, who is to be a physician," announced Elinor.

John, Fanny, Robert, and Lucy were so elated that they offered assistance for the engagement ceremony.

"Now this is what family is all about. Thank you, Lord!" said Edward.

"Yes," said Elinor. "For we will all come together very often."

14

The Letter

Isabella had finally opened all her gifts. She was amazed at all the beautiful things that she received. With all the beautiful gifts that were given, her two favorite were the brooch from Abel and the trinket box from Millie.

"Papa, I have come to help you today."

"Have you finished your project and work from school?"

"Yes, Papa, I have."

"Very well, Isabella. Take these papers, and put them in the vault."

Isabella looked at the files that her papa handed her. She was astonished at the name she saw at the top of the file. It read JOHN WILLOUGHBY.

"Papa, why are you working with Mr. Willoughby?"

"He asked for my help. Even if I believe him to be reprehensible, his concern is not. Apart from that, he may have a reasonable situation within the law."

"I have spoken to Millie, Papa, and she is a very sad girl. She has informed me that her mother and father argue all the time. She also told me that they do not love her like they should. Papa, she lives in a sad house. I wish that she may live with us."

"Dearest, according to the law, children must live with their parents unless the child is being harmed."

"Papa, she is being harmed by the situation in her home and their neglect of her."

"Dearest, I speak of physical harm."

"Papa, is causing harm to her feelings just as bad because one carries it with them forever?"

"I understand your view, dearest, but the law is what it is until someone changes it."

"Well, then, let us try to change it, Papa! Do not laws change all the time. You have friends in parliament. Ask about to see what can be done. That man Willoughby should not have been allowed to sire children. All he does is hurt people."

"Well, dearest, let us put him aside and continue our duties, shall we?"

"Yes, Papa, forgive me. The sun will be going down soon. Do you want me to close the vault?"

"No, dearest, I have a bit more to do before I depart to see Colonel Brandon. If you will, ask Henry to make my horse ready when it is time."

"Yes, Papa, I shall.

"I must go upstairs to get my things ready for the colonel. I will return shortly."

"I will put the files in the vault, Papa!" yelled Isabella.

Isabella gathered all the files that were to be put in the vault. The last file that she picked up had the name of John Willoughby on it.

"I hate you for how you are treating Millie," she said to the file.

As she was putting the files in, something was preventing them from going in. *What is it with these files? Go in right now!* She pulled them out and saw that there was something preventing them from going in. She put her hand in the vault and grabbed the envelope that was causing problems.

This envelope has my name on it. Let me see what this is.

She carefully opened the envelope and found a letter to her. As Isabella read the letter, her eyes widened as if she saw a ghost:

My Dearest Isabella,

Please forgive me for no longer being with you. Oh, how I desire to be with you forever my sweet girl. You have been the best that I have had in my life. I will always be with you in your heart.

I have asked Colonel Brandon to watch over you and to do what is best for you as he did for me. You can put your full confidence in the colonel, dearest.

I do need to let you know that you have a father. My regret is telling you that he left us when he found out that I was carrying his child. I never saw him again. I later was given information of his whereabouts from the Colonel.

Your father's name is John Willoughby and he lives at Combe Magna in Somersetshire. Should you choose to approach him, do it carefully and smartly.

I wish you all happiness and love for all your life dearest. The Colonel has my instructions for you.

With all my love, Mama

All of a sudden, Isabella screamed and hit her papa's desk over and over again. Her heart was beating faster and faster. Tears were streaming from her eyes as she cried frantically.

"I, I must go to Abel," cried Isabella.

She remembered that her papa had his horse ready outside. She ran from the house, crying frantically, and got up on her father's horse. The letter fell out of her hand onto the ground.

Sir Linton ran downstairs, not knowing what was wrong. *Why is Isabella screaming?* he thought to himself. "Isabella, dearest, where are you?"

The front door was open, and he saw his horse was gone. Suddenly he looked down and saw the letter meant for Isabella.

"Oh dear God, oh dear God!" yelled Sir Linton. He ran to the stables and got another horse, for he felt he knew where she had gone.

* * * * *

Isabella was riding so fast that she could not catch her breath. Her long black hair flew in the wind, and tears streamed down her face. She screamed out, "You cannot be my father, you blaggard! I must see Abel! I must see Abel!"

Meanwhile, Abel and his papa were out in front of their house, looking over the new horse they purchased. Abel started to look around, for he faintly heard his name.

"Do you hear that, Papa?"

"I do, son. What is it?"

"Who is that coming down the road? Oh my lord, it is Isabella!" yelled Abel.

Marianne ran outside, wondering what all the commotion was. Then they all saw Isabella riding wildly on her father's horse.

Abel and the colonel ran to Isabella as she stopped the horse, climbed down, and ran to Abel, tired and still crying. She screamed Abel's name as he caught up with her. They came together, and she fainted into his arms.

The colonel offered to help, but Abel yelled, "No! I have her, Papa."

Abel picked her up as if she weighed nothing. He carried Isabella into the house and placed her gently on the davenport. The colonel and Marianne ran in after Abel. They were worried, for they didn't understand what was happening. Sir Linton finally arrived at the colonel's house, jumped off the horse, and ran in the house.

"Chris, how is she? Dear God, please tell me she is fine!"

"Philip, what is wrong? Why is Isabella like this?"

"Chris, she has found the letter and now knows the truth!"

"Dear God, Philip, how did this happen?"

"Get me a blanket, Mama," asked Abel.

"Philip, what letter has upset her so much?" asked Marianne.

"Yes, I also would like to know about this letter that has frightened her so much," said Abel.

"Isabella was working in my office, putting files away in the vault when she found the letter with her name on it from her mother who birthed her. Chris and I were going to show it to her next month," replied Philip.

"This does not make sense, Philip, for she knows that she was adopted," said Marianne.

"Will you tell them, Philip, or shall I?" asked the colonel.

"Get on with it, Chris," replied Phillip.

After taking care of Isabella, who was sleeping, Abel rose and listened to his father.

"Isabella is the daughter of Beth Williams and John Willoughby," said the colonel.

"What!" said Abel.

Marianne sat down carefully and now understood her special attraction to Isabella all these years. She looked up to Chris with tears in her eyes and asked, "Why did you not tell me?"

"Dearest, I did not want to bring to your remembrance of a long-ago heartache."

Abel kneeled beside Isabella, looking at her while stroking her hair and cheek. He softly told her that he was in love with her and would always protect her.

"Papa, does Willoughby know that he is her father?"

"No, son, he does not. I would rather keep it quiet for now," replied the colonel.

"Philip, what will you do?" asked Marianne.

"When Isabella is better, Chris and I will explain everything. Marianne, may she stay here tonight, for I do not want to disturb her," replied Philip.

"Of course, she may, Philip. We will take care of her."

"Thank you very much. Maybe she will forgive me one day and realize it was my wish to protect her."

Abel picked up Isabella and carried her upstairs to the guest quarters. He gently laid her upon the bed. "You are my everything, and I will never have anything hurt you again."

Marianne asked Abel if he would like to stay with Isabella. "Miss Wall will stay as well to assist her personal needs."

"Yes, Mama, I will remain with her. Thank you."

"Of course, son. It is your place to be with her at this difficult time. Your father has gone to get the doctor. Please let me know when she wakes." Marianne leaned over Isabella and gave her a soft kiss on her cheek.

* * * * *

Dr. Ricker came out of Isabella's room to report that she was physically well but urged care for her mental situation.

"Thank you, doctor. May I go in now, for I am resolved to be near her?" said Abel.

"Yes, Mr. Brandon, you may go in. Just let her sleep for as long as necessary."

"Thank you, Doctor Ricker."

Abel sat on the bed beside his beloved Isabella. As he watched her sleeping, he wondered at her beauty. Her hair was long and dark as molasses with soft curls. Her cheeks were soft and rosy. He placed her small hand gently into his while praying that this situation would no longer affect her. He felt as if he and Isabella were the only people in the world.

Sir Linton quietly entered the bedroom to look upon his daughter.

"Oh, Sir Linton, forgive me. I was just praying for Isabella."

"No need to explain, son. I have always known how you felt about our Isabella. You may stay as long as you desire, Abel."

"Thank you, Sir Linton, you are very kind. Sir Linton, how are we to take care of this situation with Isabella?"

"We will explain it all to her with love. I just pray that she forgives me and your father."

Everyone was tired, for no one had much sleep. Sir Linton fell asleep in the corner chair, and Abel closed his eyes, sitting beside Isabella while still holding her hand. Suddenly Abel felt his hand being squeezed, for Isabella was waking up. She gingerly sat up and saw that Abel was there with her. She did not notice her papa in the corner chair.

"Abel, Abel," said Isabella quietly. She grasped his shoulders and hugged him tightly as he did her. Sir Linton saw what was happening but said nothing, for he has known that they love each other.

"Oh, my darling Isabella, how are you feeling?"

"I am hungry. Why am I at your house, Abel? Oh, I remember now. Abel, do you know of me?"

"Yes, dearest, but nothing has changed. You are still Isabella Linton as you should be."

"It is all coming back to me, Abel—that letter, the horse, my shame."

"Dearest, you have nothing to be ashamed of, I promise."

A deep voice came from the dark corner, which startled her a bit.

"Dearest, how are you feeling?"

"Oh, Papa, I am so sorry to have caused you to worry. What are we going to do about that letter?"

"What do you mean, dearest?"

"If that man finds me to be his daughter, he may take me away from you."

"No, my dearest. He cannot because the adoption is final, and you are now of age."

"Oh, thank God for that! I am feeling tired again. I believe I may rest till morning."

* * * * *

The next morning was fresh and new with great possibilities.

"Abel, Papa and I must go home now, for we need to have a discussion."

"As much as I do not want you to leave, I understand, dearest."

The colonel walked into the room to see about Isabella.

"Isabella, dearest, it is wonderful to see you up and well."

"Thank you, uncle. Papa and I must go home. Thank you so much for keeping me well. Will you come to our house today so we three may have our discussion?"

"Of course, dearest."

"Chris, may we borrow your barouche so we may hitch our horses to them for our journey home?"

"Most assuredly, Philip, and anything else that may be of help to you, my friend."

"Thank you very much, Chris, for all you and your family have done."

Isabella went to the colonel and embraced him as well as Abel. Her gentle touch and smile gave them peace.

After saying their farewells, Isabella and her papa were on their journey home. She put her arm under his and her head against his shoulder. He kissed the top of her head gently. Isabella and her papa understood that all would be well in time.

15

Love from Tragedy

It was a warm summer evening in July. The air was perfumed from the lavender bushes. The moon was full and gave a beautiful glow to the evening. The colonel and his family were keeping company with Sir Linton and Isabella. There were many stories told which produced much laughter, which was desperately needed. Young love was in bloom between Kennedi, William, Isabella, and Abel. Miss Wall was hurriedly coming from the house with a worried look on her face.

"Sir Linton, Sir Linton!" yelled Miss Wall.

"What is it, Miss Wall?"

"Sir, Bakerby is here from Combe Magna at the urging of Mrs. Schremmer. Mrs. Willoughby is in a grave condition and has asked for you to come."

"Right away. Get my barouche ready."

"Papa, please may I go with you, I must see if Millie is fine?"

"Very well, dearest, but hurry!"

"Papa, I will follow behind Sir Linton," said Abel.

"Very well, Abel. Take care."

* * * * *

Sir Linton, Isabella, and Abel finally arrived at Combe Magna. Mrs. Schremmer came out to meet them.

"Sir Linton, Mrs. Willoughby needs you desperately!"

"Mrs. Schremmer, where is Millie?" asked Isabella.

"She is with her mother, Miss Linton.

Sir Linton, Isabella, and Abel walked down the dim-lit hallway to where Mrs. Willoughby and Millie were. They all went in the bedroom and looked upon a truly ill woman. Millie was sitting in the chair next to her mother's bed.

"Isabella, you have come. I am so glad to see you!" said Millie.

"I am also glad to see you, Millie. Have you been out of school because of your mama becoming ill? Where is your father?"

"He is with the fox hunt in Sussex and has been gone for two days now."

Isabella had secretly prayed on the way that Willoughby would not be at Combe Magna.

Slowly and with great difficulty in breathing, Sophia asked Sir Linton to come closer, for she has a directive for him.

"Abel, you and Isabella, come here, for I need you for my witnesses."

"Sir Linton, I, Sophia Gray Willoughby, do declare to be of sound mind. My directive to you, Sir Linton, is for all my estate, property, and monies to be put into a trust for my daughter, Millicent Willoughby. Is that well enough, Sir Linton?"

"Yes, Sophia. I just need your signature if you can."

"Yes, I will demand it of myself, for he gets nothing!"

Sophia looked very frail and close to passing, but she found enough strength to ensure that her husband will leave empty-handed.

"Millie, my child, I am sorry for not loving you as a mother should. Sir Linton, please, please find someone good to keep my daughter, for her father must not."

Millie lowered herself to her mama and kissed her on the cheek. You could see a smile on Sophia's face as she gave her last breath. She would suffer no longer, said the physician, for the consumption had let her go. Isabella walked over to Millie and embraced her for comfort. As Isabella was comforting Millie, she suddenly realized that she was comforting her little sister. What a wonderful feeling she felt.

"Papa, may we take Millie home with us, for she has no mama or papa to keep her?"

"Yes, dearest, that is a fine idea. We shall also bring Mrs. Schremmer for Millie."

Mrs. Schremmer packed both her and Millie a bag enough for three days. Sir Linton left a letter for John Willoughby explaining the current situation.

The next morning, Sir Linton was writing up Sophia Willoughby's directive for leaving all property and monies to her daughter, Millie, in the form of a trust to be given at age nineteen. Sir Linton, Abel Brandon, Isabella Linton, Mrs. Schremmer, and Doctor Wellbourne were to be witnesses to what was said by Sophia as her dying declaration. So now, any previous edicts on behalf of John Willoughby were null and void.

"Good morning, Papa," said Isabella.

"And to you, dearest. Where is Miss Millie?"

"She is still sleeping. I did not want to wake her, for she looked so peaceful. Papa, I have a question. When may I tell Millie that she is my sister?"

"Not yet, dearest. Let us get this directive in place and then will come the funeral. Let me think on it, for this needs to be handled delicately."

"Very well then. I will just enjoy being with her. Papa, Millie told me that her father left for his fox hunt on Monday last knowing full well that Mrs. Willoughby was very ill. Millie said that he had no reservations about leaving, for there would be people around to take care of her. Here it is Friday, the day after her passing, and no correspondence from him. That to me seems so coldhearted. It is no wonder that her mama did not want him anywhere around Millie. We must do everything possible to protect her, Papa."

"Yes, dearest, it is coldhearted. I will ensure that she will be well protected even from her own father."

Papa, you do realize that he will try to argue against you over Mrs. Willoughby's directive."

"I have that situation, my dear, well at hand. Do not worry your pretty head on it."

"Thank you, Papa. I am now off to the kitchen, for I am very hungry.

"Oh, Isabella, I have made arrangements for Mrs. Willoughby's funeral with Edward. He agreed to officiate."

"Thank you, Papa. That is a good plan."

As Sunday was here, everyone was in agreement to coming for the funeral. They all wondered if Willoughby would appear for his family. When it was ended, everyone sighed with relief, for Willoughby never appeared.

Millie was still residing with Isabella as that was her only solace. Sophia Willoughby had been buried now, so decisions must be made for the good of Millie.

A dinner after the funeral was given in remembrance of Sophia by Sir Linton at Linton Park. It was at the behest of Isabella, for she wanted this for Millie's benefit.

The dinner was to be outside in the rose garden near the lake with aromas of roses, jasmine, and honeysuckle. There was a slight breeze with very fine weather to enjoy. Edward had requested that all his family be in attendance for lack of family on Sophia's side. There was not a bit of hesitation on anyone's part that was asked to participate, for the Ferrars and Dashwood families were favorable in their responses. Everyone came out of concern for Millie. They all desired for her to feel comfort and love. As they were finishing their meal, Mrs. Schremmer came and told Sir Linton quietly that Mr. Willoughby was at the house and waiting for an interview. Sir Linton asked Mrs. Schremmer to bring on Mr. Willoughby out slowly.

Isabella, Millie, the colonel, and Abel were called by Sir Linton to be by his side while he speaks to Willoughby.

"Millie, your father is here and on his way out. I would like you all to stand beside me as I speak with him. Are you all in agreement?"

Everyone nodded as they watched Mrs. Schremmer walk Willoughby from the house.

"Sir Linton, I am here to thank you for helping my family during this time."

Millie stood beside Isabella, holding her hand tightly.

"Mr. Willoughby, have you been to the cemetery to visit your wife's grave?" asked Sir Linton.

"No, sir, I came straight away here from my home after being aware of the situation."

"Do you not find it necessary to have visited your wife's grave first, sir?"

"Well, I will do so shortly. I see you have assembled many guests for her remembrance."

"Yes, all here are to give comfort and assistance to Millie."

Willoughby stood alone and feeling uncomfortable due to being looked upon by familiar faces in a sour manner. "Well, Sir Linton, I must take my daughter now and be on our way."

"Certainly, Mr. Willoughby, but which daughter are you referring to?"

Everyone stood shocked at Sir Linton's question.

"I am sorry, but what are you asking?"

"I shall ask again, John. Which daughter are you referring to?"

"Why, Millie, of course."

All of a sudden, Isabella let loose of her papa and Millie. She went and stood directly in front of Willoughby. Everyone stood silent and shocked, for all the attention was now on Isabella.

"Sir, do you remember running away from a woman with child by the name of Beth Williams near nineteen years past?"

Willoughby stood there like a statue with the look of fear on his miserable face.

"Miss Linton, why are you asking this manner of question? I believe that this is of no concern to you!"

"Oh, Mr. Willoughby, this is very much my concern. For you see, I am the daughter of Beth Williams, the lady that you abandoned. You left us with nothing and cared not for what could have happened to us. To make it more clear, I am your birth daughter that you abandoned!"

Willoughby resembled a ghost and could not respond immediately. Millie could not believe her ears. She ran to Isabella with tears in her eyes.

"Isabella, are you in earnest? Are we really sisters?"

"Yes, my little darling, we are sisters."

Millie did not leave Isabella's side, not even to greet her father.

"This is a desperate mistake!" yelled Willoughby.

"No, sir, it is not a mistake!" spoke Colonel Brandon. "I knew Beth very well as I knew her mother, Eliza. You, sir, are a blaggard for having left a lady in need. Beth told me of her acquaintance with you and named you as Isabella's father. Everyone has known for years as to what you have done. You have injured several people standing here today. Sir Linton and I will make sure you never hurt anyone again."

Everyone at the remembrance knew of Willoughby's disgrace but did not expect Isabella and Colonel Brandon to outright confront him. All the Brandons, Ferrarses, Dashwoods, Mrs. Jennings, Sir John, and the rest stepped forward toward Willoughby like a small army to let him know that they are there to protect the girls.

"Well, I am not going to stand here and be attacked by a mob. So, Millie, let us go now!"

"No, Papa, I am going to stay with my sister, for I have nothing left at Combe Magna."

"I will leave for now, but you are mine, Millie, and you will come home!"

"No, sir, she will not, for I have your wife's written and signed permission to care for her. Mrs. Schremmer will also be staying with us, for she is the only person that has ever put Millie first," explained Sir Linton.

"I will deal with you, Linton, through the law."

"Sir, I am the law and have all the documentation necessary from your wife before her death to relinquish everything you have, for it was not yours to begin with. Now, leave my property, or Constable Jefferies will take you out."

As Willoughby was leaving, all the families were embracing Millie and Isabella. Millie finally looked happy and at peace.

"Please, everyone, we have much to celebrate, so sit and let us have our dessert. Mrs. Schremmer, Miss Wall will show you to your new room, and Isabella will show her sister to her new room, which is located beside hers."

"Papa, you were wonderful. Can we really adopt Millie?"

"Yes, dearest, if she will have us. What do you say, Millie?" asked Sir Linton.

"Yes, Papa! Is that a good enough answer?" replied Millie.

Everyone was elated and continued a new celebration for sisters Millie and Isabella.

"Philip, does Willoughby have a recourse against you?" asked Chris.

"No, Chris, he is no match against me. I have all the proper documents given to me by Sophia Willoughby that her husband knows nothing of. He is a fool with no proper education on anything important. He is schooled well on tormenting young ladies."

"Constable Jefferies, will you post two men on my property in case Willoughby desires to be desperate—just a precaution, my friend. I will take care of the charges," asked Sir Linton.

"My pleasure, Sir Linton. I will put two of my best men here."

"Also, Constable, I will need the services of two men on Tuesday next, for we will be going to Combe Magna to retrieve the belongings of Millie and also of Mrs. Schremmer. By then, I will have the 'writ of retrieval' for their belongings."

"Yes, Sir Linton, as you wish," replied Constable Jefferies.

"Thank you, Constable. Oh, and please help yourself to one of the cakes for you and your family."

"Thank you, Sir Linton!"

16

New Beginnings

It was now late in September and two months since Sophia Willoughby's remembrance dinner. Isabella and Millie were truly sisters and in total fulfillment with each other. The legalities were to be concluded, with the impending interview at Combe Magna with John Willoughby.

Many plans were being arranged by the Ferrarses, Brandons, and Lintons. Fanny, John, Robert, and Lucy had remained sincere and affable with their families as promised.

"Isabella, Millie, hurry, ladies, for school will not wait. Your barouche has been waiting on five minutes now."

"Coming, Papa," said Isabella.

"Coming, Papa," said Millie.

Sir Linton watched his ladies run down the stairs together. His heart became full when he heard the word *papa* being called out.

"Ladies, I have an interview with John Willoughby today and will not be here when you arrive from school. I must make final your arrangement from your mother, Millie. When I return, if you desire, I will explain what was done. Do you understand, Millie?"

"Yes, Papa, I understand. Please take care, for he has a manipulative manner."

"I shall, dearest. Thank you. Have a wonderful day, ladies."

"You also, Papa," replied both ladies.

As Sir Linton arrived at Combe Magna, he noticed how lifeless it had become. After all, the last visit was with Sophia, who passed away, that very evening. After knocking on the door several times, Willoughby finally opened it.

"Well, Sir Linton, are you here for further accusations?"

"Mr. Willoughby, I am here for business on your wife's estate. Please do not make this more difficult."

"Follow me to the parlor then."

"I have papers for you to sign. The first paper is the transfer of funding from your wife to her daughter, Millicent. Sophia has put her money and property in a trust for Millicent."

"Are you going to give me my daughter back?"

"John, it was not my intention of taking your daughter. It was Sophia's dying wish that Millie is to be adopted by me."

"Really, how convenient for you. You get her and her money, which belongs to me."

"No, John, I make nothing from your wife's declaration. She felt strongly about me having Millie. She is finally very happy, safe, healthy, and loved. The only reason you married Sophia was for her money, and now you are trying to use your daughter for the same reason. That, sir, was why your wife left all to Millie. You are paying for your transgressions. You have used many people all of your life without giving back. You will have to live with that."

"Get out!" hollered Willoughby.

"Very well, but just remember—you will sign these papers, for everything has already been legally established. My visit was a courtesy and acknowledgement of you receiving all the documents. I will return when you are more affable. Good day."

Willoughby felt no shame or remorse for any wrongdoing. He believed himself to be the victim—after all, he had to endure living with Sophia and her brat, as he put it.

Willoughby was angry at the reality that he received nothing from his wife's estate. He felt he needed to clear his thoughts and find a way to get back what he felt was stolen from him.

"I must get on my horse and reflect."

As he rode wildly through the countryside, he went to all the old haunts that he and Marianne had visited. He stopped on the road in front of Barton Cottage. When he noticed Margaret watching him, he raced off, rounding the corner at a greater speed than he should. All of a sudden, a deer crossed the path of his horse, causing the horse to stop immediately, which caused Willoughby to be thrown forward from his horse onto the road. Margaret Dashwood saw the horrible accident and went to him but not before telling Melanie to go for the doctor.

As Margaret arrived, Willoughby was on the ground, unconscious and bleeding. She did not know what to do except to wait for the doctor. When the doctor arrived, Margaret described what had happened. The doctor examined Willoughby and determined that he had a broken back. He then asked Margaret to get two strong men and a backboard. After all was done, the doctor transported Willoughby to the hospital in Exeter. The news of John Willoughby spread quickly through the surrounding townships.

Sir Linton had heard the news and went to Exeter to see about Willoughby's condition. The doctor told Sir Linton that they had done everything possible but that he will never walk again. Sir Linton did not know how the girls would handle this situation. As soon as the girls returned home from school, Sir Linton called them into the parlor.

"Ladies, I have distressing news."

"What is it, Papa?" asked Millie.

"Mr. Willoughby has had a horse-riding accident. He was thrown from his horse and has broken his back. He is currently at the hospital in Exeter. The doctor advised me that he will remain there for two months."

"Oh my! I am happy that he is getting help and not dead," spoke Millie.

"Yes, I am in agreement with Millie," replied Isabella.

"Well, my little ones, I just wanted you both to be informed."

"Thank you, Papa."

"Do not forget, ladies, for we have a birthday celebration on Saturday next for Abel and Addison."

"Oh, I cannot wait. It will be wonderful," said Isabella.

* * * * *

The long-awaited day had arrived, for it was the birthday cele-bration for Addison and Abel at the Brandons'. The house was dec-orated beautifully. Out front were many barouches indicating polite society, for the Brandons would not be in association with first circle snobbery. Walking through their house gave one a glimpse of good times to be had. The smell of Jasmine led one to the large outdoor pavilion drenched with honeysuckle and wisteria. The lake had float-ing candles upon it, which cascaded little beams of light onto the water. Eight large banquet tables were lavished with all sorts of culi-nary delights from breads to exotic meats to a very sizeable cake and ice cream good enough for royalty. The presents table was adorned with yellow roses and sweet summer grasses. It was overflowing with gifts only discernible by floral paper for Addison and blue paisley for Abel. Seventeen tables, which seat twelve comfortably, were adorned with yellow roses and baby's breath sitting atop a white crisp linen tablecloth. Four large tables alone were occupied by family and close friends. All the young men were outside with Abel.

Isabella, Millie, and Kennedi were upstairs, preparing Addison for her entrance with her papa. Lots of giggling and talking of their young men occupied their time. Andrew Thomas and William Pendergrast just arrived and were anxious to see their ladies. It was an evening of promise and wonderful things to come. Marianne and the colonel were greeting their guests. Mrs. Jennings, Sir John, Mrs. Dashwood, and Margaret were all speaking on the situation with John Willoughby. It had been a month now since the dreaded acci-dent. The hospital in Exeter still kept Willoughby.

"I have always been of mind that a person who causes distress to others will surely have retribution visited upon them. It seems that Mr. Willoughby has received his," said Mrs. Jennings.

"You may be accurate in your perception of Mr. Willoughby," spoke Sir John.

"I had wished harm to him when he caused suffering to my Marianne, but I desired to release that feeling when she was finally happy with the colonel," said Mrs. Dashwood.

"I am very happy to see our young people in love. I expect there to be weddings very soon. Oh, happy day," remarked Mrs. Jennings.

"Addison, this is your papa. May I come in?"

"Yes, Papa, I am ready for you. Is Mama ready for Abel?"

"Yes, dearest, she waits for us with Abel. Ladies, get into position with your bouquets. My dearest Addison, you are very beautiful this evening."

"Thank you, Papa, for all you and Mama have done for us."

"My pleasure, dearest. Let us go now."

The birthday celebration for the twins, Addison and Abel, was fantastic. Everyone was having a wonderful time celebrating and enjoying friends and family. Kennedi and William were strolling by the lake and preparing plans for their wedding. Addison and Andrew were sitting together on the swing, enjoying each other. Isabella and Abel were sitting on the grass by the lake, for she wanted to give Abel his present in private.

"I took my time and gave your present much thought, so here it is."

"Oh, Issy, it is wonderful. I do not have a pocket watch."

"Look on the inscription in the cap."

Abel began to read:

I will love you to the end of time.

Love, Issy

"This is my favorite part. Thank you so much. I will wear it always."

"You are most welcome."

Abel reached for Isabella's hand and gave it a gentle kiss. "Issy, I have two and a half more years under your papa's tutelage, then I will be a barrister working with your papa."

"That is wonderful, Abel. I am very happy and proud for you."

Isabella gazed around to see the beauty of the night. She looked to the pavilion and perceived her papa, Millie, the colonel, Mrs. Brandon, with several others looking down to her and Abel.

"Abel, why are we being looked upon by so many?"

Abel stood up and gently took Isabella's hands to help her up.

"Are we going for a stroll, Abel?"

All of a sudden, Abel was down on one knee, looking up to his Issy, and began to speak.

"My darling Issy, you have been my best friend since we were children. I love you with my whole heart and do not care for a life apart from you. It would be my great honor if you would marry me."

Isabella was taken by surprise. Her eyes started to water with tears of joy, for she knew her heart belonged to Abel—now and forever.

"Yes, my sweet Abel. I will marry you."

Abel stood up and gave his Issy an embrace that warmed her heart and body.

Meanwhile, the onlookers at the pavilion were aware of what was happening and were filled with joy.

"How wonderful!" said Mrs. Dashwood. "We shall now have two weddings to plan for."

Kennedi, William, Brody, Addison, Millie, and Andrew all ran down to congratulate the happy couple.

"Isabella, you and I will have much to plan for our weddings," said Kennedi.

"Have you chosen a date for your wedding?" asked Isabella.

"Yes, William and I have chosen July 15th."

Isabella! I have a delicious notion! What if we were to both be married on the same day!"

"That is a wonderful suggestion, but I must speak to Abel first."

"I do not mind," said Abel as he walked up behind Isabella.

"Thank you, dearest."

"I am finally to have a sister," said Addison.

"Yes, you will, Addison. For now, I will have two sisters," replied Isabella.

The table which contained Fanny, John, Robert, Lucy, Mrs. Dashwood, Mrs. Jennings, and Sir John was busy with chatter of recommendations for the newly engaged couples. Talk of tea ceremony, engagement ceremony, and the wedding itself brought out the best intentions from the whole family and friends. The evening ended with much love and adoration.

* * * * *

It was early Monday morning when Sir John had a notion to visit Willoughby at the hospital in Exeter. He would also take a chance on asking his daughters if they would want to accompany him.

"Ladies, I am going to Exeter to visit Mr. Willoughby. Would you ladies have an interest in going?"

Millie and Isabella looked at each other for answers. Finally, one spoke.

"Papa, I will go with you just to be charitable," said Millie.

"I will also go, Papa, not for my sake but for Millie's."

"Very well, ladies. Go and prepare yourselves, for we leave in thirty minutes."

On the journey to Exeter, Isabella and Millie had a discussion as to who would speak to him. Sir Linton would again endeavor to have Willoughby receive, understand, and sign the papers. After all, it was simply a formality and gesture of goodwill. Sir Linton could just leave the papers with Willoughby, but he wanted to do what was appropriate.

"Ladies, you need not speak to him if you do not desire. He may not be affable."

"Papa, we are not fearful of him. He cannot disable us, for we are secure," replied Isabella.

The Lintons had arrived at their destination. It was a large hospital with a hefty black iron gate around and a large nameplate which read HEAVITREE HOSPITAL. Sir Linton inquired as to what room Willoughby was in. The three of them walked down a long white corridor with blinding lights from above. They finally arrived at room 153. As they went in, they observed a disheveled man sitting in a wheelchair looking out the window.

"Excuse me, Mr. Willoughby, I have come to inquire on your situation and to deliver your papers as was attempted before."

Willoughby slowly turned his wheelchair to face his visitors.

"Well, Sir Linton, come to get your pound of flesh? I see you brought my daughter—or should I say daughters. Isabella, I see myself in you, for the character of your eyes are from me."

"That is Miss Linton to you, sir. My resemblance to you is an unfortunate circumstance which I must tolerate, but my solace is that I look much like my mother, which makes me content."

"Yes, well, so be it. Millicent, do you not have any words for your papa?"

"Sir, I have come to the understanding that the word *papa* is one filled with love and care, both of which I did not encounter from you. The manner in which you treated my mama revealed to me the degenerate nature that is you. I finally have a true and loving family and will thank God for it every day. I do wish you well, for that is in my nature."

Both the girls turned and walked out, for they could not stand to be around Willoughby.

"Well, Linton, I see you have turned my family against me as well as relieving me of my estate."

"Mr. Willoughby, your wrongdoings are of your own making. The sooner you understand, the sooner your mental and physical healing will manifest itself. I am not required to have your signature, but now I leave these validated documents with you. A stipend has been given to you as a gesture of good will. Use it wisely, sir. Well, my business with you has concluded, and we must be going. One last friendly suggestion—you are never again to trouble anyone in my family or my friends as your only stipend will no longer exist. Get yourself right for your own benefit."

Before leaving, Sir Linton had a discussion with Willoughby's doctor about his situation. The doctor assured Sir Linton that his progression was coming along as expected, but he would not walk again. He would soon go home and would need constant care. Sir

Linton assured the doctor that Willoughby was receiving a monthly stipend that would help take care of any charges. He also asked the doctor to advise him when Willoughby was to leave the hospital. All arrangements were to be kept confidential. Mr. Willoughby would go on with his life without interference on others.

17

Abounding Bliss

Much tribulation had encompassed the family of Ferrars, Dashwoods and Lintons. They had all overcome deaths, despair, rejection, and snobbery. In time, they all had been brought through these tribulations and became victorious. It was now their time, for their reclamation and happiness had arrived.

It was now February, and a chill was in the air. So many plans were being assembled with cooperation of Fanny, Lucy, Mrs. Jennings, Mrs. Dashwood, and, of course, the brides to be. Everyone was in agreement that each event, even though two were marrying, would be performed once. The tea ceremony would be the first to be encountered.

All the ladies were meeting at Sir Linton's house. Mrs. Jennings offered her house for the tea ceremony.

"How many guests are we to expect?" asked Mrs. Jennings.

"Well," answered Kennedi. "Isabella and I have a number of 260 ladies on our list."

"That is most perfect, for my great hall will hold three hundred guests. I have many tables, tablecloths, and chairs for all," replied Mrs. Jennings.

"That is wonderful!" replied the ladies.

Millie was tugging at Isabella's arm.

"Yes, dearest, what can I do for you?"

"Am I to be at your tea?"

"Of course, dearest, and you will be seated by me."

Millie's smile beamed from ear to ear.

"Mrs. Jennings, my papa has had me to order the tea setting and silverware. It will be here five days before the tea ceremony," said Isabella.

"Very good, Miss Isabella," said Mrs. Jennings.

"What of the flowers?" asked Fanny.

"We are still deciding on the flowers for the tea tables," replied Kennedi.

"Well, ladies, whatever flowers you decide upon, it would be an honor for Lucy and myself to present them to you," said Fanny.

"Oh, how very kind of you, Mrs. Dashwood and Mrs. Ferrars. Thank you so very much," replied Kennedi and Isabella.

Mrs. Dashwood, Kennedi's grandmama, had asked about the food and teas to be served.

"Mama and Papa will be ordering the cucumber sandwiches, scones, cakes, and pastries along with black and green teas," replied Kennedi.

"Very well," said Mrs. Dashwood. "Sounds as if all the particulars have been taken care of."

"So, ladies, our tea ceremony will be Friday, March 18th, at four o'clock," said Kennedi.

"Ladies, ladies, what of the invitations?" asked Margaret.

"Not to worry, dear. We have already chosen the pattern, and the invitations will be here on Tuesday next," replied Isabella.

Meanwhile, the colonel was meeting with Sir Linton in his office with the door closed, which he rarely did.

"So, Philip, what is the situation with Willoughby. Is he out of our lives now?" asked Chris.

"Yes. The doctor has assured me that he will never walk again. Are you aware that he was by Barton Cottage when he had his accident?"

"No, I was not, Philip, for he has no cause to be near there."

"The doctor said that after the operation, he was waking up and that he was calling out for Marianne."

"Well, she is part of his memory after all. It is of no concern, for he made his choices, and I triumphed," replied Chris.

"Apparently, he is now at Combe Magna and not very affable," said Philip.

"He better understand that if he refuses to abide by the contract for his stipend and not end up in a miserable county hospital, then he needs to reexamine every appalling thought!" said Philip.

"I am in agreement, Philip, but I sense he feels that no other choice is available."

"Why do I feel that you have more to tell me, Philip?"

"Ahh, my dear Chris, how well you know me. I have calculatedly installed an informer concealed as Willoughby's new caretaker. Mrs. Branson is her name. I have known her for many years, and she is highly regarded in both occupations. She will apprise us of any impropriety from Willoughby."

"I see that you are putting to good use your Army training."

"Indeed!" said Philip.

A soft knock is heard on Sir Linton's door. He looked upon the shadows through the glass and noticed three slim figures.

"Chris, who would you say is on the other side of the door?"

"Well, Philip, just by observing, I would say that one of the shadows belongs to me."

"Come in, ladies."

"How did you know it was us, Papa?" Isabella and Millie each took one of his knees to sit upon. The colonel's knee was then occupied by Addison.

"Papas are good at knowing their daughters—even behind doors," laughed Sir Linton.

"See, Philip, this is what family is all about."

"I am in agreement, Chris. Well, Isabella, how are your arrangements coming along?"

"Excellent, Papa. We have finished all the arrangements for Kennedi and my tea. The arrangement for our engagement ceremony is being planned in secret by Elinor, Fanny, Lucy, and Mrs. Jennings. The engagement ceremony will be on Saturday, March 26th, and apparently here at Linton Park. Were you aware, Papa?"

"Of course, dearest, but I am not aware of any arrangements. I will just be ordered about by the ladies."

Everyone began to laugh on his remark.

* * * * *

Both of the wedding dresses were being made. The flowers were on order finally, for the ladies could not decide on colors for the wedding, so three ribbons were dropped at the exact moment, and whichever touched the floor first was to be the color. Pink took the winnings, so all manner of pink would be in accompaniment with white and shades of green. The orchestra was selected, the groom's and groomsmen's formal wear was selected. Food was pre-ordered, chairs, tables, linens, silver, and glassware also taken care of. Invitations monogrammed and sent. The security was arranged, brides' and grooms' family attire on order. This wedding was to be a great and wonderful social event in which the likes of southern England had not seen. Everyone was aware of the up-and-coming marriage ceremony especially as there were to be two of them on the same day and time, which had never happened before. April 15th at three o'clock would indeed be a wonderful day.

"Let us pray that we will have fine weather," remarked the ladies.

"What of the bridal party?" asked Sir Linton.

"Well," said Isabella. "We have chosen eight bride's ladies accompanied by eight gentlemen. Addison and Andrew will lead the bridal party. We will have one flower girl, which is to be Millie, and one bearer of the rings, which is Brody's occupation. We have also decided that Linton Park is most central to all the guests, so the wedding will take place here. Kennedi and I will be spending the night together so that we may get ready together."

"Sounds like a wonderful arrangement, ladies."

"Papa, since we are to have the ceremony by the lake, may we have swans in the water?" asked Isabella.

"Of course, dearest."

"Isabella, you are spoiled. Swans in the lake," said Kennedi.

"For sure, dearest. We shall have four swans—one for each of us."

"We have swans in our lake. I shall ask Papa to bring them the night before," said Kennedi.

"Well, well, now you like the notion, Kennedi?"

"Yes indeed. They will make a lovely addition. By the way, Isabella, have you gotten a reply from Mrs. Crouch for the wedding?"

"Yes, we have. It arrived in yesterday's post as well as Miss Ozburn."

"That is wonderful," replied Kennedi.

"Papa, we have received all replies for our wedding," said Isabella.

"That is wonderful. It will be a most beautiful day."

18

Loving Papa

"There is my little sister. Where have you been, Millie?"

"In my room, thinking. Papa, I have a desire to ask you a question," said Millie.

"Of course, dearest. Come sit on my knee and tell me of your desire."

"I am not certain on how to ask this of you."

"Millie, you may ask anything from our papa," said Isabella.

"What is it, my child?" asked her papa.

"May I put flowers on mama's grave?"

"Oh, dearest, of course you may. I reproach myself for not thinking on this wonderful notion myself. We will, at the first of every month, get a beautiful assortment of flowers from our hothouse and put them in a vase upon your mama's grave. How does that suit you, dearest?"

"Oh, Papa, how wonderful! I will go to the hothouse and look over what I may want for Saturday next. Thank you, Papa."

"My pleasure, my child."

"Papa, Millie really has made a remarkable turnabout from her previous situation since being adopted and becoming a part of our family," remarked Isabella.

"Yes, she has. We are also the better for it."

"Indeed," said Isabella.

"Well, dearest, I must go to town, for I have a special interview."

"Special interview, Papa?" asked Isabella.

"Yes, dearest, special. That is all I am going to divulge," chuckled her papa.

"Isabella!" called Millie.

"Yes, dearest."

"Look out the window."

Isabella and Millie were looking out the window in amazement. They had never seen their papa ride in a barouche alone, for he always rode his horse. The ladies' wide-eyed, open-mouth expression was incalculable. Sir Linton was well aware of his daughters watching him, which caused him to laugh.

"Isabella, why is Papa laughing with no one around, and where is he going?" asked Millie?

"I do not know, but I will investigate for his sake."

"Ladies, leave your papa alone—he has his own life to live," said Kennedi.

No sooner had Kennedi spoken than Isabella turned quickly to face her. "Well, well, Kennedi, you will share your information with us."

"What are you speaking about, Isabella?" asked Millie.

"Little sister, I do believe that our Kennedi has an awareness of Papa's special interview and will soon tell us."

"Isabella, really! I presume we have concluded our wedding list for today?" asked Kennedi.

"What, yes, of course, but you must tell us what you know about our papa, Kennedi!"

"Oh, all right! Now this may not mean anything, but I have seen your papa in the company of Miss Ozburn going on three separate occasions—once at Allenham Academy then in Exeter at the park by the courthouse and, finally, by the lake during your birthday gala."

"What were they doing?" asked Isabella.

"Well, nothing really except talking."

"So, Papa may be courting Miss Ozburn."

"I like Miss Ozburn for Papa," said Millie.

"Yes, dearest, I do also. He needs someone to care for him. It has been a long time since Mum passed on. I wonder if he went to see Miss Ozburn today when he took the barouche," replied Isabella.

"Isabella, you must not say or do anything in regard to this situation. Do you hear me?" asked Kennedi.

"Yes, of course. Millie and I will not speak of this to anyone else. We will respect Papa and wait for him to inform us in his time. Still I am excited if this is the situation."

"I want Papa to be happy," said Millie.

"I as well, little sister. He deserves it."

Isabella could not release her thoughts about her papa's happiness. She knew how much of a gentleman her papa was and must find a way to encourage the possible attachment between her papa and Miss Ozburn.

Two days had gone before a wonderful notion entered her thoughts. Isabella was to enlist the aid of her beloved Abel, for who better to move love along? Saturday next would be her weekly ride with Abel, so she would enlist his help in this romantic love tale. She must be careful not to divulge any information in front of Millie, for she was too young for such matters.

Saturday finally arrived, and Isabella was excited to meet up with Abel at their special place by their lake. Sir Linton was busy in his office and was unaware of his daughter's intention for his future love. Millie was in the kitchen with Miss Wall and Mrs. Schremmer, attempting a new menu for dinner. No one seemed to be the wiser of her plan. Everything was coming along customary for a warm and beautiful Saturday.

"Papa, I am off to meet Abel for our ride. Is there anything you need of me before I depart?"

"No, dearest, I have a bit of work to finish. Be careful, and give our boy Abel my best."

"I will, Papa. Do not work all day, for it is lovely, and you need some enjoyment away from work."

"Yes, Miss Linton. I have put away some free time for later and will make good use of it."

Both Isabella and her papa began to laugh, for she had never given him a direct order before. As she mounted Thunder, her papa's words about free time later began to stir her imagination. *What did he mean by that? Is he going to meet with Miss Ozburn later on this afternoon?* she wondered to herself. She must hurry to meet Abel so that she could begin her plans for her papa. As she reached her lake, she saw Abel spreading out a blanket for them to sit upon.

"Well, hello, dearest. You look beautiful as always."

"You are very kind, my dear Abel. I see you brought us a fruit basket and my favorite cheese."

"Yes, my lady, I did."

As Isabella sat down, she wondered on how she would approach Abel on this situation of her papa and Miss Ozburn.

"Dearest, I need your assistance on a special situation," said Isabella.

"Anything for you, my love. Is it about our wedding?"

"No, this is about my papa. I believe that he may be forming an attachment with Miss Ozburn. You cannot say anything about this to anyone."

"Well, that is wonderful. I am happy for them."

"Abel, I need to find out more on this situation. Do you believe your papa will help us? After all, he and my papa have been best of chums for many years."

"We may ask him, Issy, but be prepared to have your nose pinched," chuckled Abel.

"No, I do not believe that uncle will pounce on my nose for inquiring about my papa. I just want what is best for him and want to see him happy."

"Papa is at home right now helping to move Mama's pianoforte. We may go after we conclude our outing. Are you certain this is what needs to be done?"

"Yes, dearest. I desire Papa to have love, for he has done so much for me. I just want to make sure all is going well. Abel, do you think uncle will help us?"

"I do not know, dearest. My papa is a quiet and reserved man, but he loves you dearly and wants what is best for your papa. We can only try our best. How are our wedding plans coming along, dearest?"

"Everything is coming along most excellently. I have my dress fitting on Friday next. Kennedi and I, along with Miss Wall, have gone over our list three times to ensure all is at it should be. I believe your fitting, along with your groomsmen, is tomorrow."

"Yes, dearest. Let us pack so that we may go speak to Papa."

As they rode to Delaford to speak with Colonel Brandon, Isabella began to imagine her papa and Miss Ozburn, how happy they will be, and the children they may have.

"Isabella, Issy!" repeated Abel.

"Yes, dearest, what is it?"

"We are here. You looked as if you were far away."

"I was. I was thinking upon my papa and Miss Ozburn."

"Do not put the cart before the horse, Issy, for we know not of their situation. Let us go in, Issy, for we need to find Papa and set upon our journey for information. Do you desire that Papa be alone for our discussion?"

"No, I believe that your mama may be able to assist us."

"Very well, let us look for them. Ahh, there they are in the tea room."

"My darlings, how wonderful to see you. Have you been riding today?" asked Marianne.

"Yes, Mama. We had an outing by the lake with a delicious brunch that was ordered by my Issy. I believe she put it as practice on cooking for after we are married."

"Dear uncle, how are you getting along? Be prepared for one of my hugs."

"My dearest Isabella, I am well. How are you getting along? What brings you here today?"

"Well, uncle, I have a desire to have a discussion among us four only. You must not speak of this to Papa, for this has to do with him. I believe it to be a good situation if the particulars are accurate."

"Certainly, Isabella, but you must understand that I am not in the practice of keeping secrets from your papa. I will hear you out, dearest."

"Of course, uncle. You know how much I love Papa. I am truly blessed to have him as my papa. This is why I am here. It has come to my attention that there may be a lady who has captured Papa's attention. I want to ensure that if there be a situation between my papa and this lady, he will not be disabled by her. I have not mentioned any of this to Papa, for I do not want to disrespect him."

"Abel, what is your part in this discussion?" asked Marianne.

"I am here to help Isabella in any way I can. I too want to see Sir Linton securely happy."

"That is very admirable, son, but you, of all people, know how the heart performs," remarked his papa.

"I understand, Papa, but I too have an affection for Sir Linton and desire for him to have a much-needed happiness."

"Ahh, so we are talking to two cupids, my dear," replied the colonel.

"Dearest, do you recall how our love was established? Sometimes love deserves a little push," said Marianne.

"Very well, Isabella. What is it you desire to understand?" asked the colonel.

"Well, are Papa and Miss Ozburn seeing each other?"

"Yes. They have been in courtship since your birthday gala. I believe that they may soon have an understanding."

"That is lovely, for I like Miss Ozburn very much. I do not understand why he should keep this from me."

"Your papa knows that you have been under much tension as well as planning your wedding. I believe that he wanted to wait and see on his situation."

"Thank you, uncle. I could not have selected a better lady than Miss Ozburn. I believe that I shall wait for Papa to speak to me about his situation with Miss Ozburn."

"I agree with your resolution. He will let you know when he feels it is time."

"Well, Abel, I must return home before Papa starts to wonder where I have gone."

"Very well, Issy. Please be cautious on your journey home."

"I shall, dearest."

* * * * *

As Isabella arrived home, she noticed a barouche that looked familiar. Upon entering her home, she heard voices in her papa's office. *I believe that is Miss Ozburn*, she thought to herself.

"Papa?" she shouts. "I have returned from my ride with Abel."

"Very good, Isabella. Could you come into my office for a moment please?"

"Yes, Papa, I am coming."

To Isabella's surprise, there in her papa's office sat Miss Ozburn.

"Good afternoon, Miss Ozburn. So good to see you."

"Thank you, Isabella. I have brought you something borrowed for your wedding. It is my pearl bracelet."

"Oh, how beautiful. You are very kind. I will take great care of it."

"Isabella, come and sit with us. I would like to have a discussion with you and Millie. Ahh, here is our Millie now. Come, dearest, and sit by your sister."

"What is it, Papa?" asked Isabella.

"Well, first off, I would desire to say how happy I am that we are a family. You girls have brought much joy into my life and our home. We, however, are not complete. Miss Ozburn and I have a special attachment. I waited to tell you, ladies, when I felt it to be the correct moment. Do you girls have any remarks on this situation?"

Isabella and Millie were looking at each other with wide eyes and large smiles upon their faces.

"Oh, Papa, how wonderful. We shall have a mother now!" said Millie.

"This is wonderful news," said Isabella.

Both the girls went to Miss Ozburn and gave her large hugs. Miss Ozburn responded in kind, for she was very fond of both girls.

"Papa, may we know when you are to marry?" asked Isabella.

"Yes, dearest. Miss Ozburn and I have decided to marry in August during summer holiday. We do not want to take away from your or Kennedi's wedding."

"We are so excited for you and Miss Ozburn."

"Thank you, sweet girls. I am very excited to be part of your family. We will have many preparations. I would like for both of you to help guide me…if that is agreeable to you," said Miss Ozburn.

"Most definitely. We are jubilant for your and papa's wedding," replied Isabella.

"All will be taken care of, my little ones, but first, we must concentrate on your wedding, Isabella. Oh, one more thing, we are keeping this quiet until we have our engagement supper."

"Of course, Papa. Well, Millie and I must be off, for we have our French session with Ms. Elinor."

"Well, my dear Melanie, did I not tell you that they would be excited about our nuptials?"

"Yes, dearest, you did, for I am so happy to become Mrs. Linton."

"We shall have supper plans with close friends and family to celebrate our engagement. How does Saturday next appeal to you?"

"That is perfect. Would you like me to prepare the invitations?" asked Melanie.

"Excellent notion. I will prepare you my list so you may add it to yours."

So many plans for so many occasions. Happiness was to be abounding everywhere.

Melanie's favorite flowers were lavender and daises, so Sir Linton ensured the house would be filled with them for the engagement dinner. Isabella and Millie were busy as bees preparing everything, for they wanted all to be perfect for their papa and Melanie.

"Did everyone reply to our engagement dinner, Isabella?" asked Millie.

"Yes, dearest. Everyone that is important to Papa and Melanie will be here to celebrate with them. Millie, let us go in the kitchen and see what there is to eat. We are going, Papa. We shall see you later, Miss Ozburn. It was lovely to see you today."

"That is very kind of you both. Till later then. They are such wonderful young ladies, Philip. You have raised them in such a glorious fashion, my dear."

"I have been blessed beyond all measure, and thank God for the opportunity to have done so."

"Dearest, there is a discussion I desire to have, but know not how to approach it," remarked Melanie.

"My dear Melanie, there is not any question that you may not ask. What is it that you would inquire of me?"

"All right then, dearest. Do you have an aversion to raising any more children?"

"Not at all, my dear Melanie. Do you have a child on your mind?"

"Yes, dearest, ours."

"Ours? Well, dearest, if God blesses us with a child of our own, I will be the most fortunate man about. Is this the reply you desire?"

"Oh yes, darling, most assuredly. I am blessed beyond measure to have you with me. I have not realized what was missing in my life, for I am truly happy and look so forward to having you as my husband."

"It is I, dearest, who is truly blessed. Thank you for your love and kindness."

"Then I declare that we are both blessed and happy beyond measure."

"Hoorah, I am in agreement."

* * * * *

The day had finally arrived for the happy couple's surprise engagement dinner. The whole house was fluttering about, preparing for the guests to arrive. Isabella and Millie were elated with the prospect of having a new mother—most of all the happiness of their papa.

The aroma of lavender and daises were wafting throughout the house. The table was set with beautiful floral bone china which complemented the elegant fluted crystal glasses. There were three beautiful chandeliers sitting upon the long cherry wood dining table with matching candles the same color as the lavender. A portrait of the happy couple was commissioned specifically for this happy occasion. The portrait would be revealed by Isabella and Millie at the end of dinner to divulge the reason for this auspicious occasion.

The guests included Pastor Edward and Elinor, Colonel Brandon and Marianne, Margaret and Mrs. Dashwood, John and Fanny, Robert and Lucy, Justice Henshaw, Doctor Pendergrast, Sir John and Mrs. Jennings.

On the menu was to be roast of beef, ham, a delicious arrangement of summer vegetables, four varieties of bread, French onion soup, strawberry sorbet, and a large two-tiered cake, white, with lavender sugar flowers sprinkled about. The cake was made especially large so each guest may take a piece home. Small gifts were arranged about the cake table for each guest in remembrance of this occasion. A large selection of fine wines and beverages were on a separate table. Melanie, the girls, and Miss Wall left nothing to chance, for everything was thought out and executed perfectly.

As the guests were seated, much conversation was on the beautiful surrounding for this occasion. Everyone knew each other, therefore affording no awkward scenario. Talk back and forth was also on the ladies' tea ceremony, engagement ceremony, and the up-and-coming double wedding. Isabella and Millie were seated beside Melanie, which afforded them the opportunity for winks and smiles on the upcoming engagement surprise. The girls were so happy to be involved and felt the love toward them from Melanie. It seemed as if Millie was going to burst from happiness and impatience as she hurriedly was eating her soup.

"Millie, slow down your eating, for someone may notice your impatience," said Isabella.

"Oh, forgive me, sister, for I am very excited for what is to happen," Millie replied quietly.

"Just enjoy yourself, dearest. Take it all in, and put the memories away in your mind so that you may revisit this at any moment in the future," said Melanie.

"What a wonderful idea. I believe I shall start putting away immediately."

Sir Linton stood to declare it to be dessert time.

"We shall eat this lovely cake, but before we do, Isabella and Millie are on surprise duty. Ladies, go ahead."

All the guests turned to face the ladies standing by a covered canvas. Everyone seemed excited to see what was beneath the satin cloth. The guests were silent, for they were waiting on a speech. Papa nodded for Isabella to commence her discourse.

"Ladies and gentlemen, we are gathered here today with you, dear folk, to celebrate the beginning of an arrangement long time coming. Millie and I invite you all to congratulate the happy couple and their impending marriage in August. Millie, go ahead and remove the satin cloth carefully."

Millie's face was beaming with excitement as she removed the cloth to expose the beautiful portrait of her papa and Miss Melanie. Everyone looked at each other and the happy couple. The whole room stood up and clapped at their elation of the situation at hand. Hugs and kisses and loving words were surrounding the happy couple, for a better match could not be found. Millie suggested they all watch the couple cut the first slice of their cake. This was a perfect evening of merriment, congratulations, and sharing of future plans.

"Thank you, Philip, for a wonderful engagement ceremony. It was perfect in every way. Now it is time to concentrate on Isabella's wedding."

"No thanks necessary, darling. It was my pleasure doing this for us. I look forward to when we may have our own wedding. You are correct when you suggested we put our efforts on Isabella and Abel's wedding. What a wonderful time this will be."

19

The Weddings

Time seemed to have quickly gone by after the tea and engagement ceremonies. Not only was Isabella excited about her own wedding but her papa's also. These next two days would bring a flurry of activities. Thank God for Miss Wall and Mrs. Schremmer. If not for them, Isabella would be lost.

Isabella sat at her window seat, looking out at the wagon after wagon of china, glasses, vases, chairs, tables, and much more being brought into the house. She began to daydream about all the situations that have happened in her life. She wondered what would have become of her if her papa had not adopted her.

"Isabella? Ahh, there you are, dearest. What is the matter?" asked her papa.

"Oh, Papa, I was just thinking upon the many blessings that I have been given since you adopted me. I would have been lost without you and Mum. I love you so very much, Papa."

"No need for tears or thanks, dearest. It has been my honor and pleasure to be your papa. I have always loved you from the moment that your mum and I saw you. We knew that you were to be our little girl forever."

"Papa, I am to be married in two days and will leave our home forever. I will not see you every day like now."

"Yes, dearest, for you shall start a new life with your husband, Abel, and carry with you all the love and kindness that was given to you. Do not worry—you will still see me often. I was going to wait and surprise you with this after the wedding ceremony. As a wedding gift, if you desire, I will give you and Abel five hundred acres here on Linton Park as well as build you a house of your choosing. So you see, we will see each other very often. I have spoken with Abel about this, and he is in agreement. I asked him not to advise you, for I wanted this to be a surprise. You see, my dearest, I too want you near us— just as family should be. What are your thoughts, Isabella?"

Isabella wept with tears of joy while in her papa's arms. "Papa, your extraordinary kindness…thank you for loving me so much."

"My dearest Isabella, no thanks are needed, for you have made my life worth living. Now dry those beautiful eyes, and let us go find your sister."

"Papa, this house that you desire to build for us, may I make a recommendation?"

"Of course, Isabella. What is it you desire?"

"I want to be close enough to see your house from our bed-chamber window every time I wake. I also desire to be close to the water so that I may see and hear the waves from the back window and balcony of our bedchamber. I suppose that would put our bedroom on the second floor back corner. It will be strange, Papa, leaving the only home I have ever known and loved."

"Dearest, you will make many more lovely memories with your husband. I also fully expect to have my beautiful grandbabies visit us all the time."

"Oh, Papa, I have not thought of that. I pray that I may be a wonderful wife and mother."

"You will, dearest, for your heart is of extraordinary stock. Abel is also full of love and kindness, so no need to worry. We shall all take part in bringing up your babies."

"Papa, will you want to have children with Miss Melanie?"

"If God wills it, yes, dearest. Melanie and I have spoken on it, and we are of similar mind."

"Oh, Papa, that is wonderful! Think on it—both our babies being raised together. This is truly going to be a happy family for all time."

"Most definitely, dearest. Now if you not have anything else to speak about, let us go find our little one."

"Very well. I believe we shall find her in the kitchen. She loves being in there with Cook and Miss Wall. I believe she may become a master chef when she grows up—as long as she does not eat everything she cooks."

Both Isabella and her papa laughed heartily with the thought of seeing a large white cap on Millie's head while cooking. As they walked downstairs, they saw Millie receiving gifts from a courier.

"Look, Isabella, wedding gifts have been arriving all day. I wish I could look inside. Some carry a lot of weight. I have tallied 214 thus far. Can we open them now, sister?"

"No, Millie. It is customary to open them when we return from our wedding tour."

"What—how long will that be?"

"Well, we will be abroad for one month."

"One month! I cannot wait that long. Where are you and Abel going on your wedding tour?"

"Abel's parents have given us our honeymoon trip as a wedding gift. We are to leave the day after the wedding on the ship called *King George*. The ship takes us to France, Spain, Italy, Greece, and then return home to England. We are to have the royal wedding tour suite. I was told it has four large rooms on the upper floor."

"How exciting, Isabella! I am so happy for you and Abel."

"How about we open a few gifts—of your choosing—before we depart? Will this make you happy?"

"Oh, dear sister, yes, it will. Thank you."

"My pleasure, little one. Now, have you been to your final fitting yet?"

"Yes. Mrs. Finney made me the most beautiful lace dress with puff sleeves."

"That is wonderful, Millie. I want you to be happy."

"Have you spoken with Kennedi about the wedding?" asked her papa.

"Yes. Kennedi is busy getting her items in order. She said that Brody has agreed to delivering the grooms' rings at the ceremony.

Kennedi will be arriving here tomorrow, for she will spend the night with us. This makes things much calmer for us both since the wedding and reception will take place here."

"Pastor Edward will be arriving soon, for he is bringing the four swans. I would have liked to have seen how my friend managed catching and securing them. I am sure feathers flying about was involved," laughed Sir Linton.

The day before the wedding brought more excitement. All the dresses and the men's attire had been delivered. The food and decorations were also being delivered. Millie was busy downstairs securing the continual arrival of gifts. She watched as all the helpers were setting up the tables, chairs, flowers, and the beautiful double arbor which would be surrounded with flowers for the brides and grooms to stand under. Parson Edward would be performing the ceremony as a personal favor to both brides.

"Papa, Papa, where are you? Pastor Edward, Colonel Brandon, and Addison have arrived," called out Millie.

"My dear Chris, how are you doing today? Edward, I see your four feathered friends in the wagon," laughed Sir Linton.

"Yes, lord. Philip, you should have seen Brody and I chasing these devils around the grounds. It took almost an hour to capture these beasts, but I had to fulfill our Kennedi's desire," said Edward.

"Well, rest yourself, and I will have my men take the wagon around to the lake and deposit them." "I have brought Addison and all her bags, for Isabella wanted her to spend the night. It is shocking how many bags are needed for a wedding," said Colonel Brandon.

"Oh, Papa! I must have all these things, for it is to be a grand occasion. Greetings, Uncle Philip. Where may I find Isabella?" asked Addison.

"She is upstairs, dearest. Go on in, and I will have your bags brought up."

"Thank you, uncle."

"Well, here comes the other bride-to-be along with her many, many bags," laughed Sir Linton.

"Philip, I see a flurry of activity surrounding your home," said Edward.

"Most definitely. I long for the days of peace and quiet," said Sir Linton jokingly.

"Who is this now riding up the road?" asked Chris.

"We will find out soon enough," replied Sir Linton.

"Sir, Linton, my name is Jacob. I have been asked to bring this wedding present to Miss Isabella."

"Thank you, Jacob, but who are we to thank for this gift?" asked Sir Linton.

"I do not know, Sir Linton. There is a card attached for reference. Well, I must be off," said Jacob.

"That seems very odd. What does the card say, Philip?" asked Chris.

"Well, let us see what is written."

Dearest Isabella,

I wish this gift to be of your liking. Much happiness and health to you and your husband Abel. I would have liked to have brought the gift myself, but circumstances dictate otherwise. Perhaps we shall see each other again someday.

Your estranged father,
John Willoughby

Sir Linton's demeanor changed from elation to anger.

"That blaggard! How dare he do this."

"Philip, is that gift from Willoughby?" asked Chris.

"Yes, it is!

"Oh my. How can he do something like this? What are you going to do, Philip?" asked Chris.

"I will put it in my office for the moment. Isabella cannot know of this. I do not want her to become unsettled."

"Philip, you must advise her of this, for hiding it will be unfortunate if she were to find this out," said Edward.

"Yes, Edward, I am in agreement, but it will not be until they return from their wedding tour. So, Edward, Chris, are we all in agreement to not speak on this till the time is right?" asked Sir Linton.

"We are in agreement with you on this matter, Philip. Now, how about a brandy and cigar to celebrate the up-and-coming weddings?" said Chris.

Sir Linton, Colonel Brandon, and Parson Edward all went inside to the office to relieve their minds of this situation.

Kennedi, Addison, and Millie were upstairs in Isabella's room.

"So, ladies, how are you feeling today?" asked Addison.

"I, for one, am feeling a bit unsettled. Tomorrow my whole existence will change. I will soon be moving into a strange house with my new husband," said Kennedi.

"I am feeling the same. Abel and I will be on our wedding tour for one month. When we return, we will be living in the cottage on the other side of the lake until our house is built. Papa is gifting us five hundred acres and is building our choice of house."

"That is wonderful, Isabella. Kennedi, where will you and William live?" asked Addison.

"William's papa has gifted us the house just built down from his office on Henshaw Road."

"You two ladies are very blessed and will certainly be happy," remarked Millie.

"Thank you, dear sister. Kennedi, shall we put on our wedding dresses for our Addison and Millie?"

"Yes indeed."

There was a knock at the door. It was Miss Wall and Mrs. Schremmer.

"Come in," said Millie.

"Oh, ladies! You both look so lovely. Tomorrow will indeed be a wonderful day," said Miss Wall.

"Thank you," said Isabella and Kennedi.

"Ladies, our four-page checklist is complete and looked over three times. All that is needed this moment is the bridal parties," said Miss Wall.

"It is now dark, and all of you need to get your sleep, for tomorrow will be here very soon," remarked Mrs. Schremmer.

"Very well. Ladies, find your sleeping places, and let us get some sleep," said Isabella.

"Kennedi, what will your parents be gifting you and William?" asked Addison.

"I do not know, for it is to be a surprise to be revealed at our reception."

"Isabella, what time will our coiffeurs be arriving?" asked Addison.

"They both will be here at ten o'clock. We will need to awaken at eight o'clock so that we may have our baths. Then our cosmetic matrons will arrive at one o'clock. It is to be a busy day tomorrow. Now, ladies, it is nine thirty, and we must sleep, so good night, all."

* * * * *

The wedding day had finally arrived. The whole household was running about, ensuring that all would be perfect. All the ladies were upstairs, making themselves ready. The coiffeurs had arrived and were setting up to do Kennedi's and Isabella's hair. Miss Melanie had arrived early to help in any way she could. Sir Linton was at the stables, choosing which four horses would be pulling both wedding barouches. The double arbor was filled with the perfume of jasmine and lavender. The white padded chairs, all five hundred of them, were neatly placed near the arbor. The four swans borrowed from Pastor Edward had acclimated themselves to their surroundings. The grounds had been manicured to perfection. The perfume from the rose garden arrangement would serve as the guided walkway to the lake area where was to be the wedding venue. All the servants had been given new formal serving attire. The large freshly cut grassy area, of the west end, served as the station for all the many carriages that would be in attendance. Several judges, doctors, lords, barristers, and Prime Minister William Pitt were some of Sir Linton's elite first circle in attendance along with many friends and family of the brides and grooms.

The ladies in the wedding party were getting themselves ready in the east wing while the gentlemen were occupying the west wing. Both Sir Linton and Parson Edward, as per tradition, were to have a private moment with their daughters prior to the ceremony. As Sir Linton and Parson Edward ascended the stairs to Isabella's room, they were quiet with reflection, for giving their daughters to another brought some feelings of loneliness. They finally reached Isabella's bedroom door and knocked, calling out their daughters for their private moment. Isabella and Kennedi both appeared at the door, excited about seeing their papas.

"Papa, it is good to see you," said Isabella.

"Ladies, may we go to your parlor for our discussion?" asked Parson Edward.

"Of course, let us go. Come, Kennedi, our papas desire to have a discussion with us."

As Kennedi and Isabella were seated, their papas were standing on ceremony for this wonderful situation. First, Parson Edward offered up a prayer for love and health on both the couples. Then Sir Linton offered his wisdom to the ladies on a happy marriage.

"Isabella, Kennedi, both of you have been brought up in happy and loving homes. You must carry that foundation with you, for thinking on your husband above yourself will bring much joy and reciprocation. We have also spoken to your soon-to-be husbands on this same matter. Edward and I fully approve for your choice for husband and believe these two marriages to be blessed beyond measure. Therefore, we are here to give you both a symbol of something that has stood the test of time and grown into a much beautiful object."

Both papas walked over to their daughter and kneeled by their side, offering each of them a small rose-colored velvet box.

"Papa, what a beautiful box this is," said Isabella.

"Isabella, on the count of three, we shall open these beautiful boxes," said Kennedi.

"One, two three!" offered Edward.

The ladies were speechless, and their eyes were full of excitement. Both of the ladies hollered at the same moment, scaring their papas. They then ran to their papas with hugs and kisses, thanking them over and over.

"Well, ladies, I believe we have done very well with our gifts. What is your impression, Philip?" asked Edward.

"Yes, Edward, I am in agreement with you."

Both the ladies were at the mirror, admiring their two-carat diamond earrings.

"Thank you so very much, Papa, for now I understand your words on 'standing the test of time.' These are very beautiful," said Isabella.

"Papa, I could not have thought of a more meaningful and beautiful gift. You both have exquisite taste. Thank you so very much, and we love both of you immensely," said Kennedi.

"You both are very welcome. Now you both must finish what there is left to do. Our guests are starting to arrive. We will come and fetch you both when it is to be the time for walking you," replied Sir Linton.

"Very well, Papa. Thank you."

The ladies returned to Isabella's room where all the ladies were in a flurry to get their formals on. Millie walked in with pencil and pad to announce the final counting of presents.

"Sister, Kennedi, I believe I have the final tally on your gifts. Isabella, you have 276, and Kennedi, you are equal with her. I noticed a present in Papa's chair, but there was not a card with it. I will inquire as to whom it belongs. Oh my! Look at your earrings, and how they sparkle. You both have the same set," observed Millie.

"Yes, dearest. Our papa gave these to me, and Uncle Edward gave Kennedi her set during our father-daughter interview."

All the ladies were gathered around Isabella and Kennedi, admiring the beautiful diamond earrings nestled on their lobes.

Melanie had informed the wedding party that the weather was perfect and beautiful for their ceremony. "Ladies, your papas have informed me that all the guests have arrived. The gentlemen of the wedding party are currently downstairs as well as your papas. You must ready yourselves for your procession, for we are ready," stated Melanie.

"Line up, ladies. Kennedi, you go first and stand by your papa at the bottom of the stairs. Isabella, you are next. You shall also stand by your papa. Now when you four reach the altar, your papa, Kennedi, will take his place as parson. Your papa, Isabella, will be seated by Melanie in the front seat. You both will then stand by your grooms and let the ceremony begin. Both of you look beautiful," remarked Miss Wall.

"Are you ready, Isabella?" asked Kennedi.

"Yes, I believe I am."

As the ladies were locked arm in arm with their papas, both were also looking about with amazement at the number of guests and all the beauty surrounding them. The ladies then looked to the altar where their grooms were waiting. All four of them locked eyes with each other and realized the love between them. As the ladies finally approached the altar, both William and Abel remarked about their brides' beauty. Everyone realized that they were meant for each other.

Parson Edward officiated beautifully even though his voice seemed to waver a bit and a small tear ran down his cheek, for his little girl was now married. It was seen that Papa Linton had his handkerchief in his hand during the whole ceremony. Melanie would caress his arm to give him comfort. Each of the couples recited their own vows with tenderness and beauty. Several guests were seen to be crying with happiness, for they loved these two couples. When the ceremony finished, they walked back down the aisle as cheers and clapping erupted. The ladies were now known as Mrs. William Pendergrast and Mrs. Abel Brandon. As the guests went for refreshments, the couples were to change from their formal attire to their celebration clothing.

"What shall I call you, husband, now that we are married?" asked Isabella.

"Call me whatever your heart desires."

"Very well. I shall call you Abel in public and darling in private."

"Is it well with you that I call your Issy in public and sweetheart in private?"

"It is well, my darling Abel."

"Isabella, Abel! Are you both ready to go downstairs to greet our guests?" asked Kennedi.

"We are ready. Let us do this."

As the couples came out from the house, everyone began clapping again. The couples went to their wedding table to wait on their dinner, for they had not eaten all day. There was enough food and drink to go around twofold. When Sir Linton and Pastor Edward put on a wedding, they did it in a grand manner. Millie was nestled in with her papa and Melanie at the parents table. She looked so happy and beautiful in her dress. Both sets of parents were busy with happiness and chatter of future grandchildren. Kennedi and Isabella were dancing with their new and handsome husbands. One can surmise by looking at the two couples that the love between them was genuine and the perfect foundation for a happy marriage. As the couples were now seated at the bridal table, Pastor Edward and Elinor were making their way to the couples.

"Kennedi, dearest," said Edward. "Your mother and I are here to bestow upon you and William our wedding gift. You and William will set sail with Isabella and Abel tomorrow for your wedding tour. William, I have spoken with your papa about the amount of time you will be away, and he is in agreement."

"Oh, Papa, how wonderful! Thank you so very much."

"Yes, Pastor Edward, thank you very much for this great gift," said William.

"You are more than welcome," replied Elinor and Edward together.

"How exciting it will be for us all to be together on this journey," said Isabella.

"William, you and I must pack immediately, for time is running out," said Kennedi.

"I believe your parents have already secured your attire for your journey, dear lad," said Abel.

"You knew about this, Mr. Brandon?" asked Isabella.

"Only just now, for there was no time to apprise you, dearest," replied Abel.

"Hmmm, good answer, dearest."

They all had themselves a good laugh, for Isabella and Abel behaved like an old married couple. The wedding celebration soon started to wane as the guests were filled with joy on the whole celebration.

* * * * *

Morning had brought with it great weather for sailing. Both couples were preparing to leave for port. Millie had requested that her papa drive Isabella and Abel as well as herself, for it will be bitter-sweet having her sister gone for weeks.

"Isabella, I have your and Abel's final recommendations for your house and expect to break ground on Monday next. I shall have a full crew working six of the seven days, and expect a great amount to be accomplished by the time you both return."

"Oh, Papa, that is wonderful, is it not, my dear Abel?"

"Yes indeed. How far from your home will our house be, Sir Linton?"

"It will be 150 meters between our houses."

"That is wonderful. We shall be able to see each other frequently," said Abel.

"Do not forget, Papa, that our windows to our bed chamber must face your house as well as the sea. Both will be a splendid sight as we rise in the morning and go to bed in the evening."

"Yes, dearest, as you requested. Your house will be half as large as mine, as per your specifications. You will have five bed chambers, so I expect those to be filled with grandbabies."

"Oh, Papa," said Isabella as she blushed.

"We have arrived" stated Millie.

"Oh my, the *King George* is an immensely large ship," said Isabella.

"Look, there is Kennedi and William," hollered Millie.

"Fantastic! We are all here," said Abel.

"Let us go and get you aboard. Remember, you are to be in the Princess Anna suit," remarked Sir Linton.

"Well, Papa and dear Millie, I am going to miss you both immensely. I shall bring you both a present from every port." Isabella embraced her papa and Millie tightly.

"Love you both very much. We will see you both in a month."

"Let us go over to William and Kennedi and prepare for our journey. We shall see you soon, little sister. Sir Linton, thank you for everything," remarked Abel.

"Good and safe journey to all four of you children. Keep each other well. Love you all," said Sir Linton.

Both couples were now on the *King George* ship and off on a wonderful journey. Sir Linton and Millie were on their way back home. As they arrived, Melanie could be seen getting out of her barouche with a large picnic basket.

"Melanie! How wonderful to see you," hollered Millie.

"And you as well, my little darling."

"Philip, I brought us a large celebratory dinner to be eaten out of doors on our favorite quilt."

"Dearest, what a kind thought. I am very hungry. Millie, get a hold of the quilt, and let us walk to the lake, for we are to dine alfresco this fine evening. Oh, Melanie, everything looks divine. Take my hand, and let our dinner begin."

"Papa, what does *alfresco* mean?"

"It means that we are to eat out of doors, dearest."

"Oh, how wonderful. The next time we decide to eat out of doors, I too shall say 'alfresco.'"

"Perfect," said Melanie.

"Let us sit and feast on this culinary delight," remarked Sir Linton.

20

The Scare

"Papa, how much longer before Isabella comes home?"

"Dearest, they have only been gone one week. They still have three weeks left on their journey. Millie, ask Miss Wall to fetch me the coldest compress she can find."

"What is it, Papa?"

"I am not feeling my best, dearest."

"You have been working too hard, Papa, and have not given yourself any rest. Let me go and fetch your compress and bring you water also."

"Thank you, my little one. You are the best."

Millie quickly ran to the kitchen to fetch the cold compress from Miss Wall. Sir Linton sat at his desk with a feeling of uneasiness. He had not an understanding of why he felt hot and cold at the same moment. He called out for Millie, but there was no response. Miss Wall returned with Millie only to find her papa unconscious on the floor.

"Papa, Papa!" screamed Millie.

"Millie, go find Jackson and tell him to fetch Dr. Pendergrast immediately! We must get your papa up and lay him on the davenport. You remove his shoes, and I will remove his tie and loosen his collar. Give me the compress, for he is burning up."

"Oh, Lord, please do not take my papa away from me. Please, Papa, wake up and be well."

* * * * *

"Here is Doctor Pendergrast, Miss Wall," said Jackson.

"Ladies, let me at Sir Linton, for I must examine him."

"He has been working very hard, Doctor Pendergrast, with no rest or appetite," said Miss Wall.

"I have seen this before. Jackson, help me get him up to his bedchambers, and put on his nightclothes. Miss Wall, here is a list of my needs. You must have Jackson go to my house and have my wife retrieve these items and come back quickly."

"Yes, sir, as you wish," said Miss Wall.

Millie sat in her papa's chair with her knees to her chest with thoughts of what happened to her mother. She was crying and rocking back and forth. Mrs. Schremmer came in to console Millie and help her through this difficult time especially since Doctor Pendergrast requested she remained apart from her papa. Miss Wall has requested Jackson go fetch Melanie, for she needed to be here for Sir Linton. Everyone was very concerned over Sir Linton and were doing everything necessary for his comfort and healing.

"Millie, dearest, I want you to understand why you need not be by your papa's side. He has an infection, and I desire that you not be infected," remarked Doctor Pendergrast.

"Oh, my poor papa," wept Millie.

"Do not trouble yourself, little one. I will help to heal your papa."

"Thank you, Doctor Pendergrast. I do understand your concern and will pray that my papa will be healed."

Three days went by with the entire household under Doctor Pendergrast's instruction. His fever remained, but not as high in temperature as before. Millie remained with cook in the kitchen to help her not feel so helpless. Washing sheets and blankets were done every day for sanitary reasons. Cook prepared several different broths with homemade crackers every day for Sir Linton. The windows were to remain open to let fresh air through the house. Doctor Pendergrast told the household that even as ill as he was, Sir Linton's stubbornness reared itself. He demanded that no one was to inform Isabella or anyone outside of his house about his condition. Melanie had also been distraught during this time, for the doctor asked her not to see Sir Linton while he still carried a fever.

Finally, on day 7, Sir Linton's fever had left him, and he had regained some of his strength. The whole household had been rejoicing on hearing this wonderful news on Sir Linton's condition. Doctor Pendergrast was now allowing people to see Sir Linton.

"Papa! Oh, thank God you are better. How I have missed you."

"There is my little one. Come and give me a hug. This feels wonderful. I have surely missed you, dearest."

"Everything will be just fine now. I have prayed for you every day. Oh, there is someone else who desires to see you, Papa."

"Melanie, darling! I am so happy to see you. Please do not cry, my dear, for all is well again."

"Philip, dearest, you gave us all such a fright. Tell me that you are feeling better, for I cannot stand to be away from you again."

"Yes, dearest. Doctor Pendergrast told me before he left that all is well."

"How wonderful. Now we may have a celebration dinner to your health. I already have Cook making us a wonderful meal."

"This meal will be a welcome change from the usual broth that I have been drinking. I believe that I have lost some weight, Melanie."

"Yes, darling. That comes from not eating regular food, but you still look wonderful. Philip, are you intending on telling Isabella of your illness?"

"Yes, dearest. I think it best to be honest with my girls. Besides, Millie will most likely beat me to it."

"I am in agreement, dearest. The truth is best. They will be returning in eight days, and you can have your talk ready for her."

"I am ready for my Isabella to return. I look out the window to look upon the progress of their house—looks to be coming along very well. They will be so excited to see it, for there was nothing there when they departed."

"Darling, Colonel Brandon came by two days ago to speak with you. Since the doctor told us not to mention anything on your health, I told him you were not home. He asked me to tell you that he will have the two horses ready for Isabella and Abel's stable. I believe he thought something was not right about you not being home. He is such a gentleman that he did not question me. I felt terrible about not telling him the truth."

"He will understand, dearest, when I make him aware of my situation. How have you been managing, my dear?"

"Doing well. Millie and I have been keeping ourselves busy. We went Tuesday past to put flowers on her mum's grave. We are just so thankful that God has spared you, my dear Philip."

"Yes, dearest, for I constantly give him thanks."

"Philip, let us tell Cook that we three want our dinner by the veranda overlooking the ocean. It is such a lovely evening."

"That is a fantastic notion. Millie will be elated. Let us see if she remembers to use the words *alfresco*."

* * * * *

Another week had removed itself in anticipation for the return of the newlyweds. The Linton estate had now returned to its usual situation since Sir Linton had regained his health. Isabella and Abel's house was now resembling the blueprint that was prepared by renowned architect Jonathan Ashby. Sir Linton and Millie were outside, gathering flowers from the garden for the dinner table.

"Papa, here comes Colonel Brandon to visit us."

"Philip, my old chum, and Millie, it is so good to see you both. I expect all is well on the Linton home."

"Chris, I am so happy to see you as well. Everything is now well with us. I am sorry that I was unable to receive you when you last came. I expect you understand what was happening."

"Yes, my dear friend. Melanie explained to me the reason for our separation. I am elated to see that you have regained your health. I see that you have lost weight."

"You are quite right, old chum. Eating—or I should say drinking—my food enabled me to keep my food down as well as losing weight. Nevertheless, I now feel fit as a fiddle. However, I now own clothing one size larger than before."

"Well, Philip, you look smashing. What will you tell Isabella, for she will surely notice the difference?"

"The truth of it, but I will want to wait till we arrive home."

"Oh, my dear chum, you will have to divulge that information immediately, for you know how tenacious our Isabella can be."

"Oh, and how I know," Philip replied as they both laughed.

* * * * *

The day had finally arrived for the anticipated return of the children from their month-long wedding tour. Millie was most excited, for she had been counting down the day until her sister and new brother were to return.

"Papa, Papa, where are you? We must now go, for the ship is to be here soon."

"Be patient, dearest. We have time, for it is only half past one. I have already ordered our barouche and wagon. We are waiting on Melanie to arrive, for she wants to join us in our reunion."

"How wonderful, Papa, that Melanie will be joining us. Our family would not be complete without her. How much longer must we wait until we leave?"

"We will depart at two o'clock. Ahh, here is Melanie. How was your ride, darling?"

"Very pleasant, Philip. Hello, Millie. Are you excited on your sister's return?"

"Oh yes, Miss Melanie. I am so happy that you are traveling with us."

"Thank you, my little darling."

"Let us all get on the barouche. I expect that the rest of the family will be at port to receive the children from their wedding tour. Come, Millie, you will sit with your papa and Melanie."

"Oh jolly! We are leaving."

The ride to Brentberry Docks was pleasant. Sir Linton and Melanie discussed their up-and-coming wedding in late August. The weather cooperated fully for the arrival of the ship. The Brandon, Ferrars, and Pendergrast families were all standing under the pavilion, awaiting the docking of the ship. The happy couples could be seen waving down to their respective families under the pavilion.

"There, Papa, there is Isabella and Abel. Oh, happy day. I shall wave in return so they may see us."

"Yes, dearest, and to their left side are Kennedi and William. We must wait here, Millie, for they will be directed here when they disembark. I am glad we brought the wagon for to carry their trunks."

"I wonder what they have brought us for presents from the different lands that they visited," said Millie.

"Be patient, Millie, for you must first embrace them before inquiring on any presents," laughed Melanie.

"Yes, Miss Melanie, you are right."

"Look, my little one, they are coming this way," said Sir Linton.

"Look, Abel, there is our family. I must run to them, for I see Millie jumping up and down. Oh, my little darling, it is so good to see you. How I have missed you and Papa so much."

"I have missed you more. You must not leave us this long again, dear sister."

"Papa, I have missed you tremendously. I am so elated to be back home. Miss Melanie, it so good to see you also."

"Thank you, Isabella. We have certainly thought of you and Abel often."

"Papa, you look different. Why have you lost so much weight? You are still handsome as ever, but you must tell me what has caused you to lose weight. Have you been ill?"

"Dearest, finish your hugs and kisses so we may start our journey home. I will enlighten you about myself as we travel. Abel, so good to see you, son. We have the cottage all ready for you both. Come, let us see about your trunks."

The colonel, Marianne, and Addison, along with the rest of the family, were happily engaged with many hugs and regaled stories from their journey. Kennedi and William were also engrossed with their family on stories of their journey. Plans were in the making for a large family dinner at the house of the colonel and Marianne. William and Kennedi are now to go to their new home, which was the wedding gift provided to them by Doctor and Mrs. Pendergrast. On their journey back home, Sir Linton could no longer delay his explanation to Isabella on his terrible illness. This explanation did not fare well with Isabella.

"Oh, Papa, how could you not inform us of your terrible ordeal? Would it have been such an imposition to let your eldest daughter receive notice on your illness? There is not any place on earth that I could not have gotten a report on your health."

"My darling Isabella, I was not about to ruin your wedding tour, for there was absolutely nothing that you could have done. Doctor Pendergrast put me in isolation from everyone for two weeks. Even Millie and Melanie were not to come near me. He took very good care of me at his own risk to my illness. His instructions were that no one was to be made aware of my situation, not even your father, Abel. Please do not burden yourself with what has now passed. You and your new husband are home, we are all together, and your new house is coming along nicely. Besides, Melanie will be keeping you busy with our wedding plans. So can you forgive your old papa?"

"Yes, Papa, of course. I am sorry for going on about this. I was just frightened for you. You do seem healthy with your rosy cheeks and dapper new suit."

"Yes, dearest, I am feeling much better. I must resume my duties, for I have fallen behind. Now that you and Abel have returned, will you both be capable of working with me?"

"Of course, Papa. Abel and I have discussed on that very situation during our journey. Abel has no issue with my working."

"Excellent. Abel, you and I will resume our business on Monday next, and Isabella will help Melanie with our wedding."

"Very good, Sir Linton. I look forward to it."

"Melanie, have you any new designs on your wedding?" asked Isabella.

"Yes, dearest. I have written down several ideas for us to search out."

"Very good. I am excited for you and Papa. It will be wonderful."

21

Sir Linton and Melanie's Wedding

Everyone had situated themselves back into their regimen. William Pendergrast had fully entered into his own medical practice with his bride, Kennedi, by his side. Sir Linton had fully recovered from his illness and had been working side by side with his son-in-law, Abel. Isabella and Abel's house was quickly nearing its finish. Melanie, Isabella, and Millie were preoccupied with the preparations on the Linton wedding.

"Papa, Papa! Here come to visit are Kennedi and William."

"Yes, dearest. They have come to visit with your sister and Abel on the progress of their house."

"Shall I go and fetch Isabella and Abel?"

"No need, my little one, for they are already outside and about to stroll to their house."

"Oh, how wonderful. May I go with them, Papa?"

"Of course, but stay alongside of them."

"Isabella! I am here to go with you four to visit your house."

"Wonderful. Abel, do you think it is now time to tell Millie of her surprise?"

"Most certainly. Come along, little sister."

"Surprise—what surprise? Please tell me, or I shall burst."

"Calm yourself," laughed Isabella.

"I know of your surprise," teased Kennedi.

"Abel, shall we tell her or show her?" said Isabella.

"I believe it better to show her, dearest."

* * * * *

"Oh, my darling, look how grand. It is so large and beautiful."

"How many bedrooms are there, Isabella?" asked Kennedi with a wink.

"There are six bedrooms—one for us and four for our future children, as Papa put it."

"That only makes five bedrooms, sister."

"Oh, so it does. I forgot. The last bedroom is to be for you, my dear sister, for when you come to visit."

"What? Oh Isabella, Abel, how very thoughtful of you to think on me. This must be the surprise. Oh, happy day. I must run upstairs to see it!"

"Are you forgetting something, Millie?" asked Abel.

"What am I forgetting, dear brother?"

"Do you know which bedroom will be yours? There are many rooms upstairs," laughed Abel.

"Oh, dear me. You are right. I must be patient and wait for you to show me," giggled Millie.

"Well then, let us go on up and show you your bedroom."

They were all admiring the fine wood carvings as they ascended the elegant staircase. Millie's bedroom would be the last on the right, with Isabella and Abel's bedroom on the far left looking upon her Papa's house and the ocean.

"Oh my woosh," said Isabella.

"What is it, dearest?" asked Abel.

"I am tired from walking here and then climbing our stairs."

"Are you well, Isabella?" asked Kennedi.

"Yes, I have regained my strength. So, Millie, here is your bedroom, and it also has a privacy chamber. What is your impression, dear sister?"

"Why are you crying, Millie?" asked William.

"What is it, dearest? Are you not happy?" asked Isabella.

"I am very happy, dear sister. My tears are those of joy for you and Abel thinking on me. This is such a beautiful room. Look, this window faces the ocean. I see dolphins. Thank you so much for your kindness and love."

"Nothing but the best for our little sister," remarked Isabella.

As they continued their tour, they all remarked of the wonderful work of their architect, Jonathan Ashby.

"This is our bedchamber. I made sure that Papa would instruct our architect that the windows would look on Papa's house as well as the ocean. Is it not grand, darling?"

"Yes, dearest. It is most wonderful. There is also a stable and servant's house that will be built upon completion of our house. I am to be happy when we finally occupy our home. Now we must return, for I still have much work to do, and you and Melanie are to meet and continue the wedding plans."

"Most definitely, dearest. Come along, Millie."

"Coming! I was just admiring all the rooms. Such a beautiful house. I am so happy for you both and myself."

As they were walking back to Sir Linton's house, they were admiring the grounds and the beautiful view of the ocean. Upon arriving, they saw Melanie arrive on her barouche.

"Well, we must be on our way home. Thank you for letting us tour your lovely home. You both will be very happy there," said Kennedi.

"Thank you so much. We shall see each other very soon," replied Isabella.

"Isabella, how are you doing today?" asked Melanie.

"Very well, thank you. Shall we go to the drawing room and resume our plans for the wedding?"

"Miss Wall, could you bring us some tea please?" asked Isabella.

"Very good, Miss Isabella. Would you like some cakes as well?"

"None for me, but Melanie might want some."

"No, thank you, Miss Wall. I must take care of my waist, or I might not fit into my gown. Are you well, Isabella?"

"Yes, I am a bit tired. I have been walking more than usual. Now, what is left to do?"

"Well, I have not finished the invitations. I have Philip's list, but my list will not be large, for I do not have much family."

"How many people are on Papa's list?"

"He has 150 people. I have about ten, but some are on your papa's list."

"You need not worry. Just give me what family members you have, then we will have our total."

"I have secured the flowers, music, chairs, tables, and center table decoration. I have not any ideas on the food," said Melanie.

"Oh, my dear Melanie, let me see to that, for I know what Papa enjoys. What are your favorites?"

"I enjoy the similar foods as your papa."

"Excellent. Now what about your cake? Do you have a specific preference?"

"Well, I do enjoy raspberry jams, jellies, and the fruit itself. What if we were to have a four-tier raspberry cake with buttercream royal icing decorated with flowers of lavender?"

"That sounds delicious, Melanie. Excuse me for a moment, for I must find some wafers to calm my stomach."

"Melanie, darling, here you are. Where is Isabella?"

"She has gone to get some wafers to settle her stomach."

"Oh dear. I pray that she has not caught an illness from her journey. I have to ask you a question, dearest."

"What is it, Philip?"

"I have a wedding gift that I have kept from Isabella for fear of discovery."

"Who is it from, darling?"

"Yes, Papa, who is it from?"

"Dearest Isabella, I have kept if from you due to your possible response upon opening."

"Well, let us three see what my response shall be. May I have it, Papa? There is no card, Papa. Am I to conclude that this is from none other than Mr. Willoughby?"

"Yes, dearest, it is. I put it away before your wedding. Please forgive me."

"It is fine, Papa. I understand your concern for me when it comes to that man. No need for forgiveness. All is fine. Well, let me get to it."

As Isabella carefully opened the package, there was total silence. At last she looked upon a silver picture frame.

"What is the matter, Isabella?" asked Melanie.

"I do not understand. What is this? Who is this?"

"Let me see, dearest. Oh my lord. How can he be so cruel?" remarked her papa.

"What is wrong, Philip? May I see? Who is this a portrait of, darling?"

"Papa, who is this? Why would Willoughby send me a portrait of this woman?"

"Isabella, you must remain calm. Promise me."

"Of course, Papa. Who is she?"

"This is a portrait of your birth mother."

Isabella sat on the davenport for what seemed like hours, gazing on the portrait. She traced the outline of her mother's face with her fingers as if she were imprinting it to her memory.

"Philip, how do you know that this woman is her birth mother?"

"I became acquainted with her when the colonel and I had an interview with her about the letter she wanted Isabella to have. That is when I first laid eyes on my little Isabella. She was but two years old. Dearest, are you well?"

"Yes, Papa. It is a bit of a shock but not one that can cause me to be ill. I never thought that I would ever see my birth mother, but I have her here now. For whatever reason that man has sent me this, I believe I shall keep it—not because he sent it, but because this is the only portrait I have of her. Can you both see the resemblance between us? I am so happy that I look like her and not him."

"My dearest Isabella, are you certain that you are resolved to keep this present?"

"Yes, Papa, for this does not make me unhappy. I told Willoughby that I resemble my mother more than him, for it was true and am glad of it. I will keep this in our parlor of our new home along with the other lovely portraits of our family."

"She is beautiful, Isabella, as are you. I believe you are right to keep it," remarked Melanie.

"All right then. Melanie, shall we get on with your wedding plans? Papa, would you like to remain and make plans with us?"

"I cannot, dearest, for I must meet Abel in Exeter for an interview with a client. I suggest you ladies plan away."

"Very well, Papa. Give my husband my love."

"I will, dearest. Darling, will you stay for dinner?"

"Yes, thank you, my love."

* * * * *

"So, Melanie, have you spoken to Papa on where you both will marry?"

"Yes. He suggested we do our ceremony here at Linton Park overlooking the ocean."

"How wonderful and perfect. So the food has been placed on order as well as the tables, tableware, wines, and desserts. What of your gown and those of your handmaidens?"

"I am to have you, Addison, Kennedi, Margaret, and Millie. We all have an interview on Monday next at Lady Rutherford's Boutique."

"So tell me Melanie, what color do you want for our gowns?"

"I believe a light yellow with sprays of lavender. I have asked Brody to be our ring bearer, and he accepted with great enthusiasm. I have also asked Parson Edward to officiate."

"That sounds wonderful Melanie. Now, as your papa has passed, who will walk you?"

"I have asked Colonel Brandon, and he has accepted, for he is partly responsible for our meeting as well as your papa's best chum."

"What a perfect choice."

"Isabella, where is your sister?"

"I believe she is with Cook in the kitchen."

"No, dear sister, for I am here."

"Millie, would you accompany your sister and myself to Lady Rutherford's Boutique tomorrow, for I am to choose my wedding gown and the handmaidens' gowns?"

"How exciting! Of course, I will. Thank you for including me, Miss Melanie."

"You are very welcome, dearest."

"Just think on it, Melanie—in two weeks, you and Papa will be married," said Isabella.

"Yes, indeed. I am elated on being a wife to your papa."

* * * * *

The day had finally arrived for the union of Sir Linton and Miss Melanie. The weather was perfect as if it was ordered in advance. The guests were arriving, and they admired the beautiful scenery before the ocean. Meanwhile, the wedding party were gathered together and happily awaiting the discharge of their duties.

"Oh, Melanie, you look beautiful. Papa will be in amazement of your beauty," said Isabella.

"Thank you, dearest. You may think that I am fine on the outside, but inside I am nervous."

"Calm yourself, for all will be well. Shall we go on and unite you and Papa?"

"Most certainly."

The wedding party made their way to the gazebo overlooking the ocean. As the bride came into view on the colonel's arm, Sir Linton's eyes widened with delight and happiness.

"Philip," said Colonel Brandon, who was standing by his side as his man of honor. "You are a very blessed man. Your love and happiness will grow as you take on your soulmate. I am very happy for you."

"Thank you, my dear friend. I am very excited on this new chapter in my life."

After the ceremony, everyone was celebrating the union of Sir Linton and Melanie. Happiness abounded with all the friends and family surrounding the happy couple.

"Sir Linton, do not worry on our work, for I will be happy to continue with the business whilst you and Melanie are on your wedding tour," said Abel.

"That is very good of you, Abel. Our wedding tour shall take us to France and Germany for two weeks. I believe you and Isabella can take care of our business."

"I will be happy to help, Papa. Be happy, both of you, and no need to worry. All will be well."

"Thank you, Isabella."

"Papa, I shall also help," said Millie.

"Of course, my little one."

"So, my dearest Isabella, how are you getting along?" asked Colonel Brandon.

"Very well, uncle. Abel and I have been helping papa with his work and the wedding. I am so happy that everything worked out perfectly."

"I am happy for your papa and Melanie. He deserves to love again. It was providence that brought those two together."

"We are in agreement with you, uncle. Abel and I were about to go to our new house. Would you and Marianne care to accompany us?"

"Most definitely. Marianne, come, for we are on our way to our son's new home."

"May we go with you?" asked Doctor Pendergrast.

"Of course—the more the merrier," replied Abel.

"Darling, feel that delicious breeze from the ocean. This is one of the reasons I wanted our house built here," said Isabella.

"It is also convenient that we can see your papa's house," chuckled Abel.

"Whatever the reason, the house and property is perfectly beautiful," remarked Mrs. Pendergrast.

"Abel, could you show our guests the upper floors, and I will reveal the ground floor."

"Certainly, Isabella."

Many compliments were expressed by the Brandons and Pendergrasts. There were several innovative features of this house due to the vision of their architect. All their guests ascended the staircase but one—Mrs. Pendergrast.

"You all go on. I will remain here with Isabella," remarked Mrs. Pendergrast.

"Very well, dearest. We shall not be long," said Dr. Pendergrast.

"Isabella, are you well? You appear a bit pale," remarked Mrs. Pendergrast.

"Well, I do feel tired. I have been working diligently with Papa's business and his wedding—not getting enough rest, I suppose. Now that all has been finished, I believe I can regain my strength."

"Very good then. If I can help you on anything, please let me know."

"Thank you, Mrs. Pendergrast. You are very kind."

"Well, here we are, dearest. I have shown everyone the entire house."

"Wonderful Abel. May we go back now?"

"Of course, dearest. Hold on to me, and we shall walk together."

As they were walking back to the house, Sir Linton, Melanie, and Millie were thanking the last of their guests for attending.

"Well, here are the rest of our family. I see you have been given the tour of the new house," said Sir Linton.

"It is most remarkable," said Marianne.

"Come here to your papa, Isabella, for I want to thank you and Millie for the wonderful wedding that you have given to Melanie and myself."

"You are welcome, Papa. Abel, Abel, I…"

"Darling! What is it? Please wake up!" shouted Abel.

Isabella had fainted upon walking to her papa. Abel quickly caught her and carried her into the house. No one had any idea of what was wrong.

"Abel, let me look at her," said Dr. Pendergrast.

"I will get a cold compress and some water," remarked Marianne.

"Darling, wake up please!"

"Isabella told me that she was very tired from all the work that she had been doing as of late," said Mrs. Pendergrast.

"Well, she has no fever, and her pulse has regained normally. Has she eaten anything today?" asked Dr. Pendergrast.

"Darling, you are back. How are you feeling? Have you eaten today?" asked Abel.

"I do not think I have eaten. I have been very busy."

"Dearest, what would you like to eat?" asked her papa.

"Maybe some chicken broth and crackers."

"I will go and let Cook know to prepare this," said Millie.

"Isabella, you will rest, eat, and regain your strength. There is nothing left for you to do."

"Yes, Papa. I will do as you ask."

"Isabella, I want you to come see me on Monday next so I may do a thorough examination. Will you come and see me?"

"Yes, she will, for I will make certain of it," said Abel.

"Abel, call on my barouche, and take my daughter to the cottage. I will have Miss Wall deliver her food when ready. She must have her rest."

"On my way, Sir Linton."

"I will find something sweet for you to eat and deliver it to you when ready," said Melanie.

"Thank you, Melanie. I look forward to it," replied Isabella.

"Doctor, what do you think is wrong with my daughter?"

"I am not certain. I will know better after her examination. She has no fever, no sweating, so that alone is good news. Let her get her rest and make certain she eats properly or as much as she can."

"We will make certain of it. During our wedding tour, Miss Wall will be instructed to look in on her and make sure she has everything she needs," replied Sir Linton.

"Come, darling, let me help you into the barouche," remarked Abel.

"Thank you, everyone, for your concern. Dr. Pendergrast, I shall come to see you on Monday next."

"Very good, Isabella. Do take care. Well, good folk, I believe it is time for us to go home. Congratulations once again, Sir Linton and Mrs. Linton."

"Thank you. Safe travels," replied Sir Linton.

"Philip, Marianne and I shall also go. If you should desire anything, Abel, while Philip is on his wedding tour, please let us know."

"Thank you, Papa, I shall."

At last Sir Linton and Melanie were off on their wedding tour. Everyone at Linton Park was making sure that Isabella was resting and eating properly.

22

Isabella's Health Concern

A week had passed since Sir Linton and Melanie left on their wedding tour. The Brandon house would be finished on their return. Everyone had made certain that Isabella had regained her strength, for it was now Monday, and her appointment with Dr. Pendergrast was upon them.

"Darling, our barouche is ready. We must go now, or we will be behind our time."

"Yes, Abel, I am ready. Let us go by our house to see the latest accomplishments. Besides, it will be faster on this road."

"Very well, dearest. How are you feeling this morning?"

"I am not as tired, but my stomach is a bit under the weather. No worries, though, for I am bringing with me my biscuits and juice."

"Darling, you cannot exist on biscuits and juice alone. I can see that you have lost weight."

"Doctor Pendergrast will fix me up just as he did Papa. Do not worry. Oh, Abel, look. Our house is nearly finished. How beautiful it is."

"Yes, my darling, but not as beautiful as you."

"Thank you, my love. I wonder how Papa and Melanie are getting along."

"Very well, I am told."

"What do you mean, Abel?"

"Well, I wanted to surprise you with your papa's telegram which I received this morning."

"Let me see it. How wonderful. Papa says that they are having a wonderful time but also thinking on us."

* * * * *

"We have arrived, Isabella. Let me help you down."

"Come in and take a seat, Mrs. Brandon, for Doctor Pendergrast will see you in a moment," said Nurse Whimsy.

"Thank you. I believe I will."

"Abel, does Kennedi not work here in this office?"

"No, darling, William has an office next door."

"Ahh. We must go by and say hello."

"Mrs. Brandon, the doctor will see you now."

"I will sit here and wait on you, dearest."

"Very well, darling."

"Good morning, Isabella."

"Good morning, Doctor Pendergrast."

"Isabella, I need you to go behind the screen and remove your clothing and apply this robe."

"Very well, doctor."

"Do not be concerned, Mrs. Brandon. All will be well," said Nurse Whimsy.

"Thank you. You are very kind."

"Come, Isabella, lie down here. I am going to gently push down on your stomach, and you advise me on any discomfort."

"All right, doctor, I am ready."

"How are you doing, my dear?" asked the doctor.

"I feel no discomfort but do not understand why I feel sick to my stomach."

"That is what I am here to find out. Nurse Whimsy, please come in now."

"Isabella, I must now do an internal exam of your pelvis."

Isabella covered her face, for she has never shown herself to anyone except for her husband.

"Good, Isabella. I need you to sit up so I may do a chest exam. I will now check your heart, lungs, throat, eyes, and your ears. Nurse Whimsy, please bring me the blood kit."

"Yes, doctor."

"How are you doing, Isabella?"

"I am a bit nervous. I have never had such an exam before."

"Well, I wanted to be through, for I need all your information possible."

"What is wrong with me, doctor?"

"You have no virus, no fever, no bites or rashes. I desire to wait until I receive your blood tests before I give you my conclusion. Your heart is strong, and your breathing is clear. It will be on Tuesday next before I receive your blood test results. I will want you to return on Wednesday next for my conclusion. I suggest you get plenty of rest and eat what you can. Will you do that, Isabella?"

"Of course, doctor. May I get dressed now?"

"You may indeed. I will speak with Abel and make him aware of my expectations for your well-being."

"Thank you, doctor. Oh, Papa and Melanie will be returning on Tuesday next."

"How wonderful. One more instruction, Isabella. I understand that your new house is to be finalized soon. You are not to move or lift anything heavier than a dress. Let the moving men do all the work. You may tell them where you want items to go, so I repeat, you are not to do any of the lifting or moving. Do you understand my instruction?"

Isabella sat with a worried look upon her face but was surely going to follow the doctor's instructions.

"Yes, Doctor Pendergrast. I shall do as you ask."

"Very good. I will also advise Abel and your papa on my instructions, for I know how stubborn you can be."

"Doctor Pendergrast! I would debate you, but you are correct on your assessment of my character. Do not worry—I will be a good girl."

"Mrs. Brandon, we shall see you on Wednesday next. Have a lovely day," said Nurse Whimsy.

"Yes, thank you. Abel, I am ready to go. May we go next door, for I want to say hello to Kennedi?"

"Of course, darling. Are you all right?"

"Yes, dearest. Did Doctor Pendergrast speak with you on my situation?"

"He did. Everyone will be advised to ensure you follow his instructions. Oh, by the way, he also told me that you are not to go horseback riding until he clears you."

"What! You must be joking."

"No, darling. He was very adamant on that instruction."

"What am I to do, just sit about like a doll on a shelf? That is not in my character."

"I understand, darling, but you must do as he asks for your sake. He is bound to find out the cause on your situation. It is for your well-being."

"Very well, dearest. I promise I will do as he asks. Now let us go and visit a bit with Kennedi."

"Hello, Mrs. Darby. Is Kennedi available?"

"Isabella! How wonderful to see you. Are you well?"

"Yes, Kennedi. I had an appointment with Doctor Pendergrast today on my stomach concern."

"Well, you were in great hands, for he is a wonderful doctor. What is his conclusion?"

"Well, he gave me a very thorough and embarrassing examination along with a blood test. He wants to see me again on Wednesday next for the result of my blood test."

With a smile on Kennedi's face, she assured Isabella not to worry.

"You must follow his instructions to the letter, my dear friend. Do not worry—all will be well. We must make plans to visit very soon."

"Yes, that is a wonderful plan. Papa and Melanie will be returning on Tuesday next. Let us make plans soon. Good to see you."

"Wonderful to see you also, Abel."

"You also. Give our greetings to William."

"I most certainly will. He is with a patient at the moment."

"Well, my dearest, we must be on our way. Shall we go by the ice cream parlor on our way home?"

"What a delicious notion, Abel. I desire strawberry."

"Then I shall have strawberry also."

* * * * *

A week had passed, and Sir Linton and Melanie were returning from their wedding tour. The Brandons' house was finally finished. Abel was making certain that Isabella was keeping her promise on all the instructions given by Doctor Pendergrast.

"Abel, we must go now and get Papa and Melanie."

"Yes, dearest, for I have already called for the barouche and wagon."

"Wonderful. Let us be on our way then. I have missed them very much.

It was a beautiful day, but Isabella thought the ride seemed too long, for she was anxious to see her papa and Melanie.

"Finally, we have arrived. Look, Abel, there they are, and they are coming this way."

"Isabella, do not run towards them. Let them come to us. Remember Doctor Pendergrast's instructions."

"Of course, my dear. Papa, Melanie, how wonderful to see you."

"My dear child, it is wonderful to see you also. You look a bit pale. Are you well? What did Doctor Pendergrast conclude?"

"Well, he said that I am to take it easy and to eat as healthy as I can. He gave me a thorough examination. I am to return tomorrow for my blood results. He remarked that everything else was fine."

"Very good, dearest. Let us get home now. Abel, how is your house coming along?"

"It is finished, and we are in the process of furnishing all the rooms. Doctor Pendergrast has instructed Isabella that she is not to lift anything heavier than a dress."

"Really—that is a strange instruction. Nevertheless, I hope that my girl is following these instructions to the letter."

"Yes, Papa, I am doing everything he has asked of me."

"Where is Millie, for I was sure she would be here."

"Millie is with Cook, helping to prepare all of us a wonderful meal."

"How lovely," said Melanie.

"Abel, how has our business been of late?"

"Doing very well, Sir Linton. Everything has been handled, and we have three new clients for an interview on Monday next."

"Excellent. Thank you, son, for carrying the business on your own."

"My pleasure."

"We are finally home," uttered Melanie.

"Yes, dearest. It is wonderful to be home."

"Papa, Papa, and Melanie! You are finally home."

"Greetings, my little one. We have missed all of you so much."

"You and Melanie must rest a bit, then we shall have our dinner meal alfresco. I have been working very hard with Cook for your return dinner."

"How wonderful, Millie. We shall be ready in a bit, then we shall eat the best dinner ever," replied her papa.

"Sir Linton, I am going on to our cottage and let Isabella rest before dinner. Also, tomorrow we have business in Exeter at two o'clock. Melanie, Isabella has her appointment of discovery on her situation tomorrow. Could you accompany her in my stead?"

"Of course, Abel, I would be delighted. We might also take in the shops if she is in agreement."

"That sounds wonderful, Melanie. I am excited already," remarked Isabella.

"Dearest, your papa and I should be back home when you are finished with the doctor and your shopping. You can disclose to us on his conclusion and then show us your new apparel which you are sure to purchase."

"You are most agreeable, my dear husband. Now let us go to the cottage so I may rest."

"Very well, dearest. We shall see you all at Millie's alfresco dinner."

* * * * *

It was now dinnertime, and the family were gathered outside under the gazebo except for Millie.

"Where is our little one?" asked Sir Linton.

"She has asked that we be seated, for she will be delivering and serving our dinner," said Melanie.

"Well, this is a special occasion. My mouth is watering already."

"Here she comes and with the wine," remarked Isabella.

"Ladies and gentlemen, I have brought a red wine for accompaniment with our roast of beef," said Millie.

"No wine for me, little sister, for my stomach is a bit upset at the moment. Everything looks lovely, but am afraid that I can only partake of the soup and bread," said Isabella.

"Dearest, is your stomach in that bad of a condition that you cannot partake on anything else?" asked her papa.

"At the moment, yes. I feel terrible on not eating the wonderful dinner for which Millie worked so diligently on. All of this looks wonderful, and I am envious of you all for being able to enjoy it."

"No worries, my dear sister, for I know you would eat if your stomach were not upset."

"Thank you, my sweet Millie. I hope you continue to cook us wonderful dinners in which time will afford me the ability to partake."

The rest of the family partook on everything that was prepared. Great accolades were given onto Millie and Cook for the wonderful meal.

* * * * *

Wednesday had arrived, and Melanie was outside with the barouche to accompany Isabella to the doctor. As they rode to town, the ladies were making plans, with excitement, on the new dresses that they may purchase.

"We have arrived, Isabella. I will let you out here as I park the barouche. I will be waiting on you to finish with Doctor Pendergrast, and then we will visit the clothing shops."

"Very well, Melanie. See you in a moment."

"Good afternoon, Mrs. Brandon. If you will take a seat, the doctor will be with you shortly."

"Thank you."

As Isabella was waiting, she was praying that her results would show that there was not anything serious. To ease herself, she would think on what color and style dress and hat she would purchase.

"Mrs. Brandon, the doctor will see you now. Follow me please."

"Isabella, how have you been feeling since the last time I saw you?"

"About the same, doctor. I am still not able to eat a full meal. Have you learned anything on my situation with my stomach from my blood test?"

"Yes, Isabella. I have good news. Your blood tests indicated no infection nor diseases of any kind."

"That is wonderful, doctor, but what is causing my stomach to feel awful? There must be something else."

"Isabella, almost every woman feels like this when she is with child."

"What!"

"You are going to have a baby in May."

"A baby? Are you for certain?"

"Most certainly. What you have is called morning illness. This will pass as your condition progresses."

Isabella sat upright with a look of fright on her face as the doctor continued his explanation.

"I have certain calming tea that you need to drink every day. You are still to be easy on yourself. No lifting, stress, and still no horseback riding. I want to set up a monthly schedule to monitor your progress. As your sickness subsides, I need you to eat better, for the baby is taking his or her nourishment from you. I will let you decide on how to inform your husband and family. So, are you excited on this wonderful baby news?"

"Oh yes, doctor. This is wonderful news. I am elated beyond words. I will do as you ask—I promise. A baby—I have never thought on that being the reason for my illness."

"I am certain that your family will be so very happy when you inform them on your situation. Do not forget to set up your monthly appointment with Nurse Whimsy before you leave."

"Thank you, Doctor Pendergrast."

"You are very welcome. Give my congratulations to your husband and the rest of the family."

"I will, and thank you again."

Isabella walked out of the office with Melanie on the promise of shopping. Melanie noticed a difference in Isabella's face.

"Isabella, are you all right, my dear? What did the doctor tell you?"

"I will tell you, but first let us go shopping in here."

"Isabella, we are in the wrong shop. This is not women's apparel. This is Cricket's Cradle, a baby shop."

"Yes, my dear Melanie. This is where I wish to shop today."

"What, why? Oh my! Are you going to have a baby?"

Yes, dearest Melanie. You must not say a word to anyone. I want this to be a surprise. I shall purchase some baby items, wrap them, and present them at the dinner table this evening."

"I am so happy for you and Abel, my dear. Your papa will not be able to contain himself nor Abel."

"I will need your help with my presentation."

"I will be happy to help you plan your surprise. Abel and your papa will want to know what the doctor said as soon as they see you."

"Everyone will have a small gift by their dinner setting this evening. I will say that the gifts are for taking such good care of me. They must all open their gifts at the same moment. I will have you put the gifts on the table right before we eat. We will get home just in time for dinner, so no one has a chance to ask me on my situation."

"That is a fantastic notion."

* * * * *

While Sir Linton and Abel were on business in Exeter, Isabella and Melanie were busy with the surprise. The kitchen was busy with anticipation of a great meal to accompany the news of the baby. Millie was not made aware of Isabella's situation due to her becoming so elated that she would not be able to contain herself. The dinner hour was approaching quickly, and Papa and Abel would be returning from Exeter soon.

"Millie, will you go and set the table for me please?" asked Melanie.

"Of course."

"Isabella, have you gotten the gifts wrapped?" asked Melanie.

"Most certainly. I will put them at the appropriate place setting after Millie sets the table."

"Melanie, darling, we are home. Where are you?"

"Ahh, dearest, you startled me. We all were in the kitchen preparing our dinner. I have asked Isabella and Abel to join us for dinner."

"Wonderful notion, darling. Let me go clean up, and we will meet you in the dining room. Oh, by the way, what did Isabella find out on her situation from Doctor Pendergrast?"

"Darling, I believe she wanted to keep that private. Maybe she will enlighten us as we eat our dinner. She seems better if that is of any help to you."

"That is good news. Well, I am going to wash."

"Melanie, do you know where Isabella is?" asked Abel.

"Oh, she is around here somewhere. You will see her soon. After you wash, you may go to the dining room, for we are about to serve."

"Yes, of course. Please ask her to find me, for I want to know of her visit with Doctor Pendergrast."

"I will, Abel."

The dining table was perfectly dressed with the best china and glassware. Each setting, save two, has a gift placed beside it. Everyone started into the dining room and is to be seated. Isabella is the last to enter the room.

"Dearest, are you all right? I have been wanting to speak with you," asked Abel.

"Yes, my darling, but first, everyone must open their gift. I bought these to let everyone know how thankful I am for how well you looked after me."

"My Isabella, always thinking on others," remarked her papa.

Isabella and Melanie sat at the table with smiles on their faces. Millie was rejoicing on the unopened present. One by one, the presents were opened. Their faces were priceless and confused at the same moment. Millie received a silver rattle with engraving which says, "From your Aunt Millie." Papa received an engraved silver portrait frame which says, "From your Grandpapa." Abel's gift was a book on how to take care of your baby. Everyone looked at Isabella as she was nodding. All of a sudden, the whole family shouted with cheers and happy tears as they made their way toward Isabella.

"Oh, my darling, you have made me the happiest man in the world. So your stomach issue is because of our baby?"

"Yes, my darling."

"My sweet Isabella, we are so happy for you both. I am to be a grandpapa. When will this blessing occur?"

"Doctor Pendergrast said in May."

"Millie, my sweet sister, why are you weeping?"

"I am to be an aunt. I have never ever been so happy in my life."

"You shall be a wonderful aunt."

Everyone was so elated that they forgot about dinner. They were all making plans for the upcoming blessing. In came cook with a large pheasant, carrots, and squash.

"Congratulations," uttered Cook to Isabella and Abel.

"Thank you, dear Cook. Please be seated and enjoy our celebration, for you have been part of family for twenty years. Where is Miss Wall?" asked Isabella.

"Here I am. What may I do for you, Miss Isabella?"

"You may sit at our table, for you also will share on our wonderful celebration."

"Celebration?" asked Miss Wall.

"Miss Wall, my daughter has advised us on her condition. In May we will be adding a new member to our family," said the proud grandpapa.

"Oh, Miss Isabella, how wonderful. Abel, I am very happy for you both."

"Thank you, Miss Wall."

Time just seemed to pass away for everyone at the table. Laughter, tears, and many plans were being shared. Isabella was so elated that she did not realize she was eating everything on her plate without any feeling of sickness.

23

Circle of Love

As it was now November, the leaves were falling, and there was a crispness in the air. The news on Isabella and Abel's impending blessing warranted a special dinner which would encompass all the family near and far. These families thrived on good news, especially where love was concerned, for it was due them.

"Miss Melanie, I have the invitations for November 25th. Are you in agreement?" asked Miss Wall.

"Most assuredly. I have ordered the food, flowers, and drink. I have spoken to Isabella on all our planning, and she is in agreement. I am excited on having our special announcement dinner at Abel and Isabella's new house."

"I am as well, Melanie," said Isabella.

"I see you are awake from your laydown," said Melanie.

"Yes, I feel better. When we planned for our house, we made certain that our dinner table would hold for certain twenty-five people."

"That is a good notion, for this family loves to have dinner surprises," said Melanie.

All three ladies began to laugh at the amount of time that was used in the planning of surprise dinners.

November 25 was currently upon Abel and Isabella. Their house was filled with workers finishing their tasks before the families arrived.

"Abel, I have not seen the finished invitation list. Do you know where I may find it?"

"Yes, darling, I have it. Here it is."

"Thank you, dearest. I see all Dashwoods, Ferrars, Brandons, Sir John, Mrs. Jennings, and the Pendergrasts. That should make about twenty-one guests or so. It is a fine notion that our table will hold twenty-five."

"Yes, darling, I believe it is. We still have six hours before our guests arrive, would you like to lay down a bit?"

"I will, dearest, but not at the moment. You had a wonderful notion on making another master chamber downstairs for my progression."

"Well, thank you, dearest. I thought the stairs would be too much on your condition. I am going to check on the grounds to ensure all is well. I will see you soon."

"Very well, dearest. I will go and see how our dinner is coming along, then I will go rest."

All the families were excited to be coming together. No one had any idea on the reason for this dinner. Discovery on this situation would be a joyful one. These families had not been all together in a season. Perhaps more joyful news would be forthcoming.

"There you are, darling. I see you have a new dress," remarked Abel.

"Most definitely. My waistline has expanded, so my dresses needed expanding also. We have one more hour before our family will be arriving. Have you seen to all the preparation?"

"Yes, dearest. All is well. Ahh, I see your papa and Melanie coming down the road."

"How wonderful. Will you ask Melanie to come visit me when they arrive?"

"Yes, dearest."

"Isabella, you look lovely. Is that a new dress?" asked Melanie.

"Yes, it is. I have had to buy several new dresses for my expanding waistline."

"I can see why. I will also be buying new dresses in a short while," giggled Melanie.

"Really? I cannot see where you have put on weight. Oh my, Melanie, are you saying that you are expecting a baby?"

"Yes, dearest. We just found out today."

"How wonderful! I am so happy for you and papa! You must announce this wonderful news alongside us at our dinner this evening."

"I believe we will. The whole family will be here to rejoice for the both of us. Isabella, you should have seen your papa when Doctor Pendergrast told us this news. He was jumping up and down like a child. It was humorous and wonderful at the same moment."

"Oh, Melanie, my heart is so full. I cannot wait to look at their faces when we make the announcements."

"Isabella! Our guests are arriving, dearest."

"Very well. We will be there soon."

All the families were sitting around the table, enjoying each other's company. Talk on business, horses, and children had everyone's attention. The clinking of a wine glass was made to gather everyone's attention. The room was silent as the host stood up to give the announcement.

"My dear family and friends, we want to thank you, dear folk, for joining us on this dinner. We also want to let you know that Isabella and I are to be expecting a new blessing in May."

Everyone began to cheer and clap on such a happy occasion. All of a sudden, Sir Linton clinked on his glass and expressed the news on their blessing. Once again, cheers resounded. As everyone was congratulating the couples, William clinked his glass with news that he and Kennedi were also expecting. More cheers and clapping all around. In between the clapping, Robert stood and clinked his glass and reported that he and Lucy would be adopting their four-year-old son in December. The room could barely contain the love, tears, laughter, and congratulations surrounding the couples. Plans on the future and talk went on for hours. Happiness filled everyone, for these families, in particular, were well deserving.

* * * * *

As time went by quickly, the month of May was now upon them. Isabella tired easily and was anxious to meet their baby. Not knowing if the baby would be a boy or girl matters not, for boy and girl names had been written down and agreed upon. If the baby was to be a girl, her name would be Katherine. If it was to be a boy, then Taylor would be his name.

"Abel, Abel!" shouted Isabella.

"Yes, dearest. What is the matter?"

"I have wet the linens and am in pain."

"What! Oh, my darling, I believe our baby may be arriving. I am getting dressed and will get Doctor Pendergrast. I will wake Millie and then go to get Miss Wall to help you. I will return soon, my love. I love you."

"And I love you. Please hurry!"

"Millie, wake up! Your sister is going to have a baby today. Go to her while I get Miss Wall to come and then go to get the doctor."

"Yes, Abel. Go! I will go to her."

"Isabella, how are you getting along? Tell me what to do!" said Millie.

"Dearest, go wake up our cook and ask her to boil a large pot of water. I also need you to bring me all the bath cloths you can find."

"Yes, sister, yes! On my way!"

Isabella was lying across the bed, moaning and breathing quickly. All of a sudden, Miss Wall burst into the room along with Sir Linton and Melanie.

"Oh my, my, my! These pains are terrible!"

"Breathe, Isabella, like the doctor asked you to do. Let me get you a cold cloth to put on the back of your neck," said Miss Wall.

"Dearest Isabella, I am here for you, but I will wait in your drawing room if you need me," remarked her papa.

"Very well, dearest. Just be aware that you and I will be going through this in July," remarked Melanie.

"Yes, of course," answered Sir Linton.

"Melanie, would you get my book and read to me, for these pains are not constant," asked Isabella.

"Yes, Isabella, of course."

"Millie, will you sit on the bed by me?"

"Of course, dear sister."

"Here comes the pain again!"

"Breathe, Isabella, breathe! said Melanie.

"The master chamber door flew open, and there was Abel with Doctor Pendergrast.

"All right, Isabella, you are doing well. I must exam you for to see how far along you are. I need Melanie and Miss Wall to stay, and the rest go to the drawing room. Abel, all will be well. You will meet your baby very soon," said Doctor Pendergrast.

The more Isabella moaned and groaned, the more Abel paced the hallway. Sir Linton was consoling Abel by telling him on Isabella's strength.

It was now daylight, and five hours had passed when a scream was heard. All of a sudden, the silence was broken with the cries of a baby. Doctor Pendergrast opened the door and invited all in to meet the new member of the family.

"Abel, go meet your baby," said the doctor.

"Oh, my darling, how are you feeling?"

"Much better, dearest. Look at what we created. Look at how much hair Taylor has," remarked Isabella.

"Taylor? That means we have a son. We have a son! He is beautiful like his mother. I am so very proud of you. He is so small."

"Come, Grandpapa, and look upon your grandson. Millie, Melanie, is he not wonderful?" remarked Isabella.

"Yes, dear sister, he is beautiful. He has so much hair."

"He is remarkable," remarked Sir Linton and Melanie.

"Abel, Isabella, I have written out two copies of his birth certificate. He is born on the thirteenth of May in 1797. He weighs almost three and a half kilograms. Taylor is excellent in every way. I have asked Miss Wall to stay and help Isabella on her personal matters. Isabella, when he starts to cry, you will need to feed him as we spoke of. Well, my job is finished. I am tired and must go home now. I will need to check on you both before the end of this month. If you should need me before this, send me a message."

"Thank you so much, doctor, and to everyone that was here for our little miracle," said Abel.

* * * * *

On the announcement of the birth of Taylor Philip Christopher Brandon, gifts arrived from all over central and southern England. Abel and Isabella were the most amazing parents.

A correspondence for Isabella had been delivered to Sir Linton's home. The sender was none other than John Willoughby. Sir Linton went to his daughter's home to deliver the correspondence. Abel, Isabella, and Taylor were in the downstairs parlor.

"Sir Linton, come to visit your grandson?"

"No and yes. I have come for a correspondence has been delivered to my home for Isabella."

"Who would send me a correspondence through you, Papa? Everyone knows I live here?"

"Well, it is from John Willoughby."

"What! He has a lot of nerve writing to her," said Abel.

"Darling, not so loud, for you will wake Taylor."

"I am sorry, dearest."

"Isabella, do you want this, or shall I burn it?" asked her papa.

"No, Papa, I will read it. Thank you."

"Are you for certain, dearest?" asked Abel.

"Yes, darling. I am curious on this correspondence."

"Very well, here it is," said her papa.

Isabella carefully opened the letter. She would read the letter in silence first.

Dearest Isabella,

By the time you receive this correspondence, I will be gone from you. Congratulations on your son. I know you will be a wonderful mother apart from me being your natural father. I know you have no confidence in me because of my impertinent conduct. I was given not once, but twice the opportunity on being a father. I reproach myself on that opportunity. I am not asking for forgiveness, for my reclamation has come and gone. I am however, delighted on how wonderful and kind you and Millie are, considering that I am or rather was, your natural father. I will use my one and only prayer on you and your sister, for it will be wasted on myself. I pray that God continue to bless you, Millie and your family.

Sir Linton and Abel stood by quietly to give Isabella the peace on reading the letter. When Isabella was finished, she gave her papa the letter. Abel noticed that she had a single tear on her cheek.

"Darling, are you well?" asked Abel.

"Yes, dearest. My sadness is on the loss of a soul and not his former position in my life. My concern now is on Millie, for she knew of him longer. Papa, will you please advise Millie on this announcement, for I believe you are the best to tell her."

"Of course, Isabella. I will take this letter and speak to her this evening."

"Thank you, Papa."

* * * * *

Two days had passed since the letter on John Willoughby. Isabella was consumed with taking care of her precious baby, Taylor. The thought of Millie had been weighing on her mind. There was a knock on Isabella's door.

"Millie, dearest, come inside. Is everything well?"

"Sister, I have been unsettled since papa informed me on John Willoughby's passing. How have you been in this regard?"

"Well, my sweet sister, I am more concerned on you. I thought it best to have papa be the one to advise you on him."

"I understand, but you have still not told me on your feeling on his passing."

"I had many feelings on him passing. At first I felt sorrow, for his soul was lost, then anger for not being a good father. At last, I felt grateful."

"Grateful? For what, Isabella?"

"You really do not know why, do you?"

"No, sister, I do not understand."

"Grateful for him giving me you. Providence brought us together. I was the happiest when I found the truth on you being my sister. This could not have happened without him. Millie, it is a miracle that we both are happy and well loved without him being part of our lives. It is also a miracle that we both were adopted by Papa. We were meant to be, despite the impertinent nature of Willoughby. Therein lies the providence."

"I understand now. Papa also spoke on providence. I am feeling much better. Thank you for being my sister. I love you."

"No thanks needed, dearest. I love you also, for we all are content within our families," remarked Isabella.

* * * * *

August was here with the hopeful continuation of happiness on each branch of all the families involved. June and July brought new souls within the families. In June, William and Kennedi received the blessing of a daughter called Catarina. Sir Linton and Melanie received their blessing in July on a son called Jacob. The whole of the families involved were to participate in the baptism of all three babies by Pastor Edward on Sunday at Delaford Parish.

"Dearest, everyone is nearly here. The parish is filling," remarked Elinor.

"Yes, my dear, I have just about finished my sermon. I will be there shortly," answered Edward.

Edward felt a strange yearning to visit his stables where Silver and Gold resided. These two horses were left to him by his mother on her will. As he caressed his horses, he reflected on his mother's words on her will of being filled with affection and having much regret in her life. His spirit was content with the sermon that he prepared for this special occasion. Everyone involved would be here today to listen and understand that their providence had been completed and rejoice in it.

Pastor Edward entered his parish and with a smile walked to his pulpit. He stood there quietly for a moment with his head bowed. He then raised his head and looked about on all the familiar faces that had risen from the ashes of despair, manipulations, greed, snobbery, and deceit. He then spoke.

"My dear family and friends, the title of my sermon is on the circle of love. When I am finished, you will understand the meaning on the circle of love. We will then conclude with the baptism of three precious souls. It has been put upon my heart and spirit to relay God's word onto each of you. We all start out in certain stations in life. What comes from that is obtained through good or bad circumstances. Providence comes as an acceptance of God's word. It has been everyone's individual choice that God gave us as to the path taken towards or away from our creator. It is not unusual to be in the same family, and each soul's circle is more fulfilled than the others. I have been witness to many partial circles even among my own tribe. It is more agreeable to our creator that your circle of love is closed and fulfilled.

"Realizing that your circle is imperfect is the first endeavor on fulfilling the closer of your circle. Knowing and understanding that your circle needs closing and not fulfilling that endeavor is being impertinent and in contrast to God. I desire to help those whose impertinence is guiding their lives even if takes a lifetime. I can sincerely say that each of you seated here today have your circle of love fulfilled. With your fulfillment come blessings, happiness, and love.

"I look at each of you and know how far you have come and that you have let go of your impertinence. I see the love in your eyes for those in your family as well as your friends. My heart is full on looking at all the closed and protected circles of love and in giving God the glory. We, as God's children, have overcome our impertinence and know how to ask God for help in the future. Let us always give thanks to God. Amen.

"It is now time for our little souls to be baptized. I ask that you, mothers and fathers, bring your babies here to bring your children into the kingdom of God. It will then be your responsibility to keep them there. In doing this, we will begin to close their circle of love."

The families gathered together for each child's baptism and realized that going forward, their retributions guided them to their fulfillment of their circle of love.

Afterword

My inspiration for *Sensible Retribution* was the book *Sense and Sensibility* by Jane Austen. The film *Sense and Sensibility*, which was produced by Lindsay Doran and directed by Ang Lee, was also an inspiration. I was impressed by Emma Thompson, who wrote the screenplay.

I wanted to build on the original characters by introducing a few new characters. They would give my story line a complete opportunity for restoration of family and love.

In *Sensible Retribution*, the social hierarchy of the Dashwood, Ferrars, and Willoughby families are to evolve for happiness' sake, making right the wrongs of these families onto each other and love interests. To bring to light the secret indiscretion of John Willoughby's illegitimate child, I wanted Isabella's journey to be in contrast to her natural father's impertinent character. Isabella is everything that John Willoughby is not. Isabella is not only surrounded by love but shows strength, loyalty, and compassion.

The evolution of those in need of retribution was not only a spiritual need but for the happy survival on each character. The families involved were made to realize that everything they have been taught was in direct conflict with God and their serenity.

Mrs. Ferrars finally realized that her impression on her children created the impertinent character onto others. Her transformation started with her son Edward—his example of God's love, impressed onto her heart, that she needed to change if there was to be any peace and love for future generations. She planted those seeds through her letters to her children—Fanny, Robert, and Edward.

Edward's character was aligned with God's love. His strength, devotion, and love would restore what was missing in Fanny and Robert. Their progression toward righteousness enabled providence to restore the Ferrars and Dashwood families.

Starting my book in church for a funeral then ending my book in church for the baptisms was to show the gifts of love acquired through God—therefore, *Sensible Retribution.*

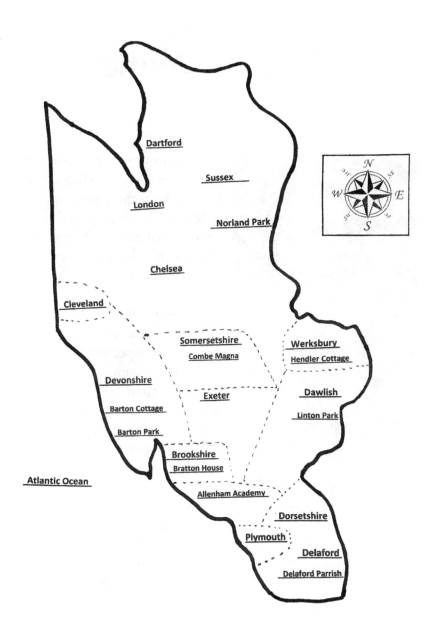

Dartford

Sussex

London

Norland Park

Chelsea

Cleveland

Somersetshire

Werksbury

Combe Magna

Hendler Cottage

Devonshire

Dawlish

Barton Cottage

Exeter

Linton Park

Barton Park

Brookshire

Bratton House

Atlantic Ocean

Allenham Academy

Dorsetshire

Plymouth

Delaford

Delaford Parrish

About the Author

Jenny Taylor's writing came to her later in her life. Being happily married for forty-three years with two children and four grandchildren, who are characters in her book, along with a thirty-two-year career in early education kept her quite busy.

She has always had a fascination with books and movies of the early 1800s, especially in Europe.

She has admired Jane Austen's book *Sense and Sensibility*. She has also admired the movie *Sense and Sensibility* many times.

She wanted a happier continuation and ending on Jane's story. The unfairness of treatment against one's own family in regard to status bothered her greatly. The cruel treatment from a scoundrel toward the women he has courted inspired her to make right his wrongs with a befitting resolution against him.

She wanted sweet love, devotion, and integrity for her book. The fitting title was *Sensible Retribution* because it captures all that is to be right and happy like the circle of love.

CPSIA information can be obtained
at www.ICGtesting.com
Printed in the USA
BVHW041242280423
663224BV00007B/303